Death Rides

a

Pale Horse

Other Western Historical Books by Dusty Rhodes

Man Hunter

(Winner of EPIC Award for Best Historical)

Shiloh

Jedidiah Boone

SUNDOWNERS
A division of
Treble Heart Books
1284 Overlook Dr.
Sierra Vista, AZ 85635-5512
http://www.trebleheartbooks.com

ISBN:1-931742-03-0

Death Rides a Pale Horse
by
Dusty Rhodes

SUNDOWNERS

A Division of Treble Heart
Books

Chapter I

"And I looked, and behold a pale horse: and his name that sat on him was death." (Rev. 6:8)

Dr. Lucien Robertson pushed hesitantly through the door to his office, turned slowly, and paused before gently closing the door. His mind whirled, still undecided as to how he would break the news to the patient sitting in front of his desk. In his thirty-one years as a doctor, he had never learned how to tell someone they were dying.

Taking a deep breath, he resigned himself to the unpleasant task that lay before him, turned, and moved wearily to the chair behind his desk. Lifting his eyes, he gazed over the top of his wire-rimmed glasses into the face of the patient across the desk.

The man before him was a tall man: sledge-shouldered, and skinny as a rail. His sun weathered skin stretched tight like a drawn bowstring over high cheekbones, making his Indian heritage quite obvious. A jutting chin sloped back towards a long, thin neck and prominent Adam's apple. On another man the chin might have looked weak, but on T. J. Littlejohn, it just looked dangerous.

His beak-like nose created an appearance that was not pleasant to look at and was enough to cause most folks to shun him. But it was those dark eyes, narrow of lid, peering from sunken sockets, which sent shivers up and down Dr. Robertson's spine.

Death, that's what you saw when you looked at T. J. Littlejohn, those eyes were the eyes of death. Not only was the man dying, he was death incarnate. Once a man laid eyes on T. J. Littlejohn they never forgot him.

"How long we known each other, T. J.?"

The reply came out in a rattled whisper. One had to listen closely to make out the words.

"Fifteen, sixteen years I reckon. You birthed all three of the youngins. Tad is just shy of fourteen now."

"How is the family?"

"The family's tolerable, and thanks for asking, but we've known one another too long to beat around the bush, doc. That grim expression on your face pretty well tells me the news you got for me ain't good. Go on, spit it out. What's wrong with me?"

"The truth is, T. J., there ain't no easy way to say what I got to say. Something's eating away at your insides. Looks to me like it started in the colon, but from what I can tell, its spread into your lungs and pretty much through your whole body. That's why you're passing blood and losing so much weight. When I saw you last spring you stood over six feet and must have weighed well over two hundred pounds. When I weighed you awhile ago you weighed one hundred sixty-two."

"Ain't there some kind of medicine you can give me to cure it?"

"I'm sorry, T. J., but there's no known cure for what you got. Someday, maybe, but right now there's just nothing I can do."

"What you saying, Doc? You saying I'm dying?"

"I'm sorry."

For a long moment neither man spoke. The patient stared in stunned silence through the window behind the doctor but seemed to be staring past the busy activities of the street outside, lost in a world of thought.

"How long I got left, doc?"

Sighing heavily, the doctor gave the only answer he could offer. "No way to know for sure, but judging by what I saw in the examination and from what you told me, I'd say no more than six months, most likely less."

Fear was the usual reaction to news that one was dying. In his years of practice, Doctor Robertson had seen it many times, but he could detect absolutely no emotion whatsoever in the eyes of this patient.

"How bad will it get before it happens, Doc?"

"You'll likely continue to lose weight. Passing blood will increase as time gets closer and the pain will intensify," the doctor said as he pushed a bottle of golden liquid across the desk. "This will help some. It's called laudanum, it's an opiate sedative. Take a swallow when you need it. I wish there was something else I could do."

T. J. Littlejohn pushed from the chair, scooped the bottle from the desk, and stuck out a work hardened hand. The two old friends looked each other in the eyes for a long minute as they shook hands.

"Thanks for telling me straight, Doc. There's some things I'll be needing to take care of. Guess I best get at it."

Sheriff George Paxton was leaned back against the wall in a straight-backed chair with his feet on the desk and snoring loudly. He awoke with a start as the door of his small office was pushed open, interrupting his usual afternoon nap. Keeping the peace in Lubbock County, Texas in 1873 was a boring job.

"Afternoon, George," the tall intruder whispered hoarsely.

"Afternoon, T. J., what brings you into town? Haven't seen you since last spring. You okay? You seem sorta off your feed."

"Had some business. Can we sit a spell? Got some things on my mind."

"Grab a chair. Want some coffee? Made it fresh couple of days ago."

T. J. Littlejohn declined the offer with a single shake of his head as he folded into a chair. He swept the office with a searching gaze. His eyes paused and fixed on the group of faded wanted posters tacked to the board wall behind the lawman's desk.

Sheriff Paxton squinted critically as he stared at the wispy shadow of the man that had been his friend for more years than he cared to remember. He couldn't believe this was the same man that he had rode side-by-side with when they fought the Mexicans together back in '46. T. J. Littlejohn had been a captain in the Texas Volunteers. He was the chief scout and best tracker in the whole regiment. He had served four years as a Texas Ranger and was maybe the toughest man George had ever known. After T. J. and Mary were married, they had fought the Apache and land grabbers and the drought to hold on to their little spread about twenty miles from town out on Yellow House Creek. *But look at him now, barely half the man he had once known.*

"How old are you, T. J."

"I'll be forty-six come spring."

What's wrong, T. J.?"

"Doc says I'm dying. Says there ain't nothing he can do. Says I got some kind of something eating my insides."

Shock swept across the sheriff's leathered face. For long minutes neither said a word. Finally, George Paxton lifted his gaze and looked his friend in the eyes.

"I'm shore sorry, T. J." George said, shaking his head sadly.

"Reckon in a way, I'm lucky. Death slips up on most folks—

catches them unexpected—they don't have time to do what needs to be done. That's what I want to talk to you about. I got a wife and three youngins out there in a shotgun shack and nothing to leave them but a patch of south Texas prairie and a handful of scrawny cows. I gotta get my hands on some money and I ain't got long to do it, that's why I come to see you."

"I'd like to help you, T. J., but I got even less than you. I barely make enough to get by. How can I help you?"

Littlejohn pointed a nod toward the posters on the wall. "Any of those still good?"

The sheriff twisted a look at the fliers behind him. His eyebrows lifted in a wrinkle as the meaning of his friend's question sunk in.

"Them? Can't say for shore, I get new ones in from time to time. Don't usually even bother to put 'em up. Hombres like that don't usually ride through our neck of the woods. Got some around here somewhere that come in not long ago, though. You thinking what I think you're thinking?"

"Except for robbing a bank, that's the quickest way I know to make some money."

"Quickest way I know to get yourself killed too. T. J., we've know one another a long time. I reckon you're the best man with that Colt pistol you're wearing I've ever seen, but the kind of men you're talking about here are cold blooded killers."

"Yeah, well, when you already know you'll be dead in a few months, a few days more or less don't seem to matter a whole bunch. How about seeing if you can lay your hands on them posters you mentioned?"

Sheriff Paxton tugged open a squeaky drawer of the dilapidated old desk and rummaged around. Finally he pulled out a stack of wanted fliers and tossed them across the desk.

T. J. took his time thumbing through the stack before withdrawing one. For a long minute he studied it carefully.

"What about this one?"

The sheriff leaned across the desk and darted a glance at the poster. "The *Sanchez* brothers? Now there's a pair of bad ones, sure enough. Way I hear they been nothing but trouble all their lives. But the straw that broke the camel's back was when they murdered a whole family over in Arizona. Somewhere near Tucson, I think it was. I've got the telegram about them here someplace."

After a few more minutes searching, the lawman pulled a stack of wrinkled telegrams from the bottom drawer, fumbled through them, and produced the one giving the particulars about the *Sanchez* brothers.

"Says here they hail from over in New Mexico, near a place called Alamogordo. If I was gonna go looking for them two, and mind you I shore ain't, that's where I'd start."

"Three hundred apiece is a lot of money," Littlejohn said, as he folded the poster and telegram and stuck it in his shirt pocket. "You reckon I could trade my team of horses and wagon for that buckskin old man Isaacs down at the livery is always bragging about?"

"That's a fine piece of horseflesh, shore enough. A man could ride far and fast on a horse like that. But Silas Isaacs is a horse trader. He's tighter than Dick's hatband to boot."

"Think I'll mosey down and try to do some trading, I'll need a good horse. Thanks George. I got to stop by the store and pick up some things. Hang on to any new wanted posters you get in, will you? And if you're out my way, I'd be obliged if you'd look in on my family while I'm gone."

"You can count on it, T. J., it's the least I can do."

The two old friends shared a warm handshake before T. J. turned and headed for the General Store.

Wiley Stubblefield glanced over a shoulder from stacking canned goods on a high shelf as T. J. entered.

"Morning, Mr. Littlejohn. It's been quite a spell since I've seen you in town."

"Yeah, need to pick up a few things."

"How's the family?"

"Tolerable."

"What can I get for you today?"

"Need to look around a bit if you don't mind."

"Help yourself. Let me know if there's something in particular I can help you with."

T. J. moved slowly through the narrow isles of the spacious store. Shelves and counters were piled high with most anything one could possible want or need. It wasn't that he was looking for anything, truth was, he was putting off doing something he had never done even once in his whole life—ask for credit.

Then he saw it, and he stopped to stare at it for a long space of time. Mary's stove. Actually it wasn't a stove at all, just a picture out of a catalogue tacked to the wall. Mary had spotted it back before Sally was born, over five years ago now, and had fallen in love with it at first sight. It was something, sure enough. White and green with silver colored legs and handles. It even had a place with a water reservoir to keep bread fresh. But the price was one hundred twenty-eight dollars. It might just as well be a thousand. She hardly ever mentioned it anymore since times were so hard, but he knew she hadn't stopped dreaming that maybe someday they might be able to afford it. But now it looked like that someday would never come.

Turning abruptly, T. J. swallowed the huge lump in his throat and the sick feeling of disappointment. Yes, and failure. Failure at not being able to give Mary something she wanted so badly. He stalked back to face Wiley Stubblefield.

"Mr. Stubblefield, is my credit good until the first of the year?"

A furrow plowed across the storekeeper's forehead and his eyebrows skewed together. His eyes crawled down the length of T. J.'s body like he was judging the worth of a steer.

"How much credit we talking about?"

"The price of one of them new Henry rifles over yonder on the rack. I've got to be gone for a few weeks and my boy needs a gun to look out for things."

"Don't see why that couldn't be arranged."

T. J. took a deep breath and let it out on a long sigh. A feeling of relief surged over him.

Silas Isaacs was a grizzled old liveryman and Lubbock's only blacksmith. Most folks would judge him as a hard man but if a fellow took the time to get to know him they learned he had a heart of gold. The rhythmic beat of his hammer on the steel anvil played a soothing sound as T. J. walked to the stable. Isaacs wore a battered old hat, leather apron, and a crooked grin that peeked out from behind a full shaggy, gray beard.

"Afternoon, Silas."

"Afternoon, T. J.," the smithy said around a mouthful of tobacco before pausing and spitting a long stream of brown liquid at a pesky horsefly. "Saw you pull in awhile ago. What brings you to town?"

"Had some things to attend to," he said, sidling casually over to the corral fence and examining the buckskin with a searching gaze. "Whose horse you shoeing?"

"That young Baker boy's sorrel threw a shoe. These young folks nowadays don't know the first thing about how to take care of a horse."

T. J. listened to the liveryman with his ears, but his mind was sizing up the buckskin in the nearby corral. It was maybe the most beautiful horse he had ever laid eyes on: At least fifteen hands tall, bright, alert eyes, thick chested, sturdy looking legs. It was the kind of horse most cowboys only dream about, the kind a man could depend on.

"I see you still got that buckskin in the corral. Ain't you found nobody to pawn that old gelding off on yet?"

"Say what? That's the best dang horse in south Texas! Show me a horse that's gaited like that buckskin and I'll show you a poky-dotted buffalo. That gelding can strike a gait and hold it till the cows come home."

"Might be getting a little old to make a man a good riding horse though," T. J. offered.

"Old? He'll outlive the both of us."

"Well, I shore wouldn't argue that point. I've been thinking about getting me a saddle horse. I just might be talked into taking him off your hands. How would you trade?"

"Depends on what you're tradin'."

"Tell you what, Silas, if you'll throw in a good short horn saddle, I'll trade you my wagon team of blacks, yonder, for the buckskin straight up."

"If you weren't such a good friend I'd take offense at an offer like that. That gelding is worth two teams."

"My team of blacks can outwork any two teams in the south plains. You still got that old twelve gauge Stevens sawed-off double-barrel shotgun?"

"Shore do. What you needin' with a gun like that for, T. J.?"

"Aw, just always kind of had a fancy for one. Tell you what Silas. What if I throw in my wagon? It's a Great Northern, and still in good shape, would you trade for the buckskin, saddle, and the shotgun?"

The liveryman swiped off his floppy hat, mopped sweat from his face with an arm, and spat another stream of tobacco, all the time obviously studying the offer.

"Sounds fair I reckon," he finally said. "Guess you got yourself a trade."

"How about borrowing one of them mules there in the corral to tote some supplies back to the house? I'll be riding back through in couple of days, I could drop it off then if that's agreeable?"

"That'll be fine."

The old man fetched a good looking saddle, bridle, and saddle blanket from a side room and hung them on the rail fence.

"Had that saddle hanging in the shed long enough," Silas said. "It needs to be put to use. Reckon it'll last you awhile."

"Long enough," T. J. commented as he caught up the buckskin and led him over to the fence. He checked the gelding's teeth. "I'm guessing six years old."

"Bout right," the liveryman said, turning the sorrel he had just shod back into the corral and spitting a stream of tobacco. "Jest broke in good."

While T. J. saddled his new horse, Silas caught and cinched a packsaddle on a Missouri-brown mule.

"Don't really need a lead rope for old Solomon here, him and that buckskin ain't been separated in years. He'll go anywhere that gelding goes. Reckon if that pale horse ran off a cliff old Solomon would trail right along behind it. Best trailwise mule I ever seen, and I've seen more'n a few in my time. Tell you one thing for shore, ain't nobody gonna be sneaking up on your camp in the night with old Solomon around. He can hear a night sound that's out of place for a hundred yards and he'll let you know about it."

"If times weren't so hard I'd try to buy him from you, but guess you'd want an arm and leg for him."

"Tell you what, T. J., with that gelding gone, he won't do nothing but keep me awake braying all night anyway, go ahead and take him. I'll throw him in as boot."

"You don't have to do that, Silas, but it's mighty decent of you. I'm obliged.

T. J. toed a stirrup and swung into the saddle. Silas handed him up the sawed off Greener. A soft leather bag full of shells was tied to the handle.

"You be careful with that scattergun. It'll blow a hole in the side of a barn you could drive a team and wagon through and it's got a kick worsen old Solomon. Where you be headed?"

"Got some business over in New Mexico Territory."

"Uh-huh. Long ride."

"Yep. Be seeing you, Silas."

"Hope so," the liveryman called after T. J as he rode away. "You take care of yourself now. You hear?"

Without looking back, T. J. lifted a hand acknowledging the farewell.

CHAPTER II

A thin tendril of smoke from Mary's supper fire trailed lazily from the rock chimney and bent sharply on a westerly breeze. T. J. reined up as he topped the hill and for a long minute sat his saddle and allowed a slow, sweeping gaze to crawl across his little valley.

Yellow House Creek funneled down from the hills and meandered its way through groves of sycamore and tall, stately lodgepole pine and cut through the heart of the wide valley. Gentle rolling hills guarded the valley on three sides and provided plenty of lush, green grass that was hock-high on the forty head of cattle that grazed peacefully below.

T. J. felt the same thrill rush through him as he had the first time he laid eyes on the valley almost twenty years ago. He had been tracking a war party of Apache when he came upon the valley by accident. It was love at first sight. He knew instantly this was where he would make his home and raise a family.

It was two years before he returned with his new bride. Mary shared the same love for the valley as he did and together they had built their little log cabin on a rise a quarter mile across the creek. A barn and smokehouse followed. They had plowed the fields, raised crops, and eventually managed to get hold of a few cows and a bull.

Over the years they had fought summer droughts, roving bands of Apache and bandits, and long, back breaking hours in the Texas sun to build a home for their children, and children's children.

Life in his little valley had been good, leastwise until now.

How was he going to tell Mary what the doctor said? How could he explain to his children? How could he make Mary understand what he was about to do and that he had no other choice but to do it?

Setting his protruding jaw firmly and with the pack mule following along closely, he touched heels to the buckskin's flanks and moved slowly down the sloping hillside toward home.

"It's pa!" T. J. heard his son, Tad shout. He saw him lean his ax against the woodpile where he had been splitting wood for the coming winter. "Ma, Pa's home!" he yelled again as he squinted into the setting sun. "He's riding a horse and leading a mule. Wonder where the wagon is?"

Four-year-old Sally was the first to burst through the open door from the cabin. Her older sister, Marilyn, followed close on her heels. Sally took one look and lit out in a beeline toward her approaching father, her bare feet carrying her swiftly through the knee-high grass. Her long, golden hair caught the setting sunlight and crowned her head with a glowing halo.

T. J. felt a surge of pride rush through him as he watched all three of his children running to meet him. He tried to swallow the huge lump that crawled up the back of his throat when the thought struck him. *I'm about to lose all this. I won't get to see my children grow up. I won't be around to teach Tad the things he needs to know to help him become a man. I won't get to see Marilyn develop into a beautiful lady like her mother. I won't be able to enjoy Sally's tiny arms around my neck and hear that small voice whisper, "I love you, papa." I can't even spend the time I have left with them. No, I have to put aside my own feelings; I have to provide for them after I'm gone. This is something I have to do, no matter what.*

Unable to control his emotions, tears betrayed him and seeped from the corners of his eyes. Reaching quickly, he swiped them away with the back of a hand before anyone saw. None of his family had ever seen him cry before. He had to be strong for them.

Sally was the first to reach him and, reining up, he leaned over and swept the small girl up into the saddle in front of him.

"I'm glad you're home, papa," the girl told him, nestling her rosy, fresh face close against his chest. "Is this horse ours? Can I guide him by myself?"

Tad ran up, excitement bubbling from his dark eyes as he examined the buckskin and mule with an admiring gaze.

"Sure is a beautiful horse, Pa. I reckon that's the most beautiful horse I've ever seen. Is he yours? Did you buy him? Where's the wagon and team?"

"Yeah, he's ours. I traded the team and wagon for him and the mule. The mule's name is Solomon. I'll explain it all to your ma later."

Twelve-year-old Marilyn reached them. She said nothing, but reached a hand to rub the buckskin's sweaty nose. T. J. was amazed how much his eldest daughter looked like her mother: same golden hair, same blue eyes that seemed to sparkle all the time, same creamy-white complexion that always looked freshly scrubbed. Both were tall and graceful, with a pert, button nose and oval features. She is going to be her mother made over.

Lifting his gaze, T. J. saw his wife standing just outside the door of the cabin wiping her hands on her white apron that partially covered a long, blue work dress. Mary's long corn silk hair, the color of the sun, hung in a plait down her back well past her waist. He had never understood what miracle brought them together. Even after eighteen years of marriage her beauty still took his breath away. How an ugly half-breed Cherokee like him could have ever won her love still bumfuzzled him. He lifted a hand. She waved back and began walking to meet him.

"Look Ma!" Sally hollered, lifting the reins so her mother could see she was guiding the horse. "Look at Pa's new horse. I'm guiding it all by myself. See Mama, see?"

"Yes, I see," Mary said, the tone of her voice and her lifting eyebrows clearly conveying an unasked question

"I'll explain later," T. J. said, swinging a leg over the saddle and stepping down. Wrapping an arm around Mary's waist he pulled her close as they walked slowly toward the house, leading the buckskin by one rein, while Sally held on to the other.

"What did you find out?" Mary asked softly, not wanting the children to hear, searching her husband's face for some sign to answer her question.

"We'll talk after supper," he told her.

"It's almost ready. I hoped you would get home in time. Marilyn and I will go finish while you see to your *new* horse."

From her tone, it was clear he was going to have some tall explaining to do after supper.

Mary Littlejohn glanced quickly around the room. Supper was over, the dishes washed and put away, and her oldest daughter was helping Tad with his numbers. Although she was younger than her brother, she was far ahead of him when it came to book learning. Sally was sitting on the floor beside her father's rocker playing with her doll.

Mary's gaze flicked again to her husband's face as it had so many times during supper, looking for some emotion, some reaction, some indication that would give her a hint of what the doctor had found out. Something was different about him since he got home but she couldn't figure out what it was. He was good at hiding his feelings, he always had been, it probably was part of his Indian heritage.

For six months she had watched helplessly as the man she loved wasted away. Despite her constant urging he had steadfastly denied there was anything wrong and refused to make the long trip into town.

"Stop worrying about me," he would say. "I'm just a little off my feed, I'll be all right."

Finally, after she had accidentally come upon him in the barn during an exceptionally hard coughing spell and noticed him coughing up blood she had put her foot down and insisted that he go see the doctor.

"T. J., this is the last straw! You're going to see Doctor Robertson if I have to hog-tie you and take you myself! It's just not normal to lose as much weight as you've lost and I've been worried sick about the blood you've been passing, and now, you're vomiting up blood. How long have you been doing that?"

T. J. said nothing, just a single shake of the head as he swiped his mouth with a shirtsleeve.

"Please, T. J., I'm begging you. Do it for the children *and* for me. Go see what's wrong with you."

He had hitched the team to the wagon and headed to town the next morning.

Now, she had waited as long as she could. She was terrified of the answer but she had to know what the doctor said. Clearing her throat to get rid of the lump that had been there ever since her husband got home, she took a deep breath and tried to calm the nervous feeling in the pit of her stomach.

"It's such a lovely evening outside," she said, in a vain attempt to disguise the nervousness in her shaky voice. "Suppose we could take a little walk?"

"Don't see why not," T. J. answered, seeming to jerk awake from a trance and flicking a quick glance at his wife before pulling himself from the rocking chair in front of the stove.

"Your father and I will be right back," she called over her shoulder as they stepped outside.

It was a beautiful fall evening. The Texas sky was putting on another of its spectacular displays. The moon was full and seemed so close one should be able to reach up and touch it. A million pinpoints of light winked like diamonds from an inky black canopy of darkness. A whip-o-will called to its mate and far off, the bark of a coyote broke the stillness of the night.

Normally, she would have thrilled at the sights and sounds of their little valley, but not tonight. As they strolled silently together a tight, dry knot of fear coiled just beneath her ribs. Suddenly she knew. The realization burst somewhere in her whirling mind. It was the silence, not words, which gave her the answer she didn't want to know. *If the news from the doctor had been good he would have already told me,* she decided. Fear migrated north from her stomach, setting her chest ablaze. Panic shot through her, stealing her breath away.

"I've got to know," she finally managed, her voice quivering. "What did the doctor say?"

For a long, breathtaking moment he didn't answer. He just walked beside her, staring absently off into the darkness.

"T. J., we have never kept anything from each other in all the years we've been married, please don't start now. We have faced some hard times before but we have always faced them together. Whatever this is, we can handle it."

They had reached a high, grassy bank overlooking the creek.

A huge oak tree with its heavy branches guarded the spot like a sentinel. Moonlight skittered across the rippling water, creating a trail of light that seemed to illuminate the whole area. It was one of their favorite spots; they had made love there many times over the years.

T. J. stopped, turned to face her, and reached to take both of her hands in his. For a long time he stared deep into her eyes as if searching her very soul. She heard him take a deep, shuddery breath, then exhale. A ripple of dread raced the length of Mary's spine and she braced herself for what was coming.

"Not this time. I have something... There's something eating away my insides. The doc says there's nothing he can do."

It took a long moment for the words to sink in. When they did, it was like a mule had kicked her in the pit of her stomach. Her knees felt wobbly and weak. Panic shot through her and stole her breath away; it took nearly all her strength just to breathe. Shattered, hollow, broken, feelings tore her insides, Mary's head began to shake back and forth in denial. She felt her eyes go wide. Tears breached her eyelids and scorched a hot trail down both cheeks.

"No. No. It can't be. It just can't!" She heard her own words escape her lips in a half scream. "Please, God, *no!* Don't let this be happening."

In her dazed and confused state, she was only half aware when T. J. gathered her into his strong arms and pulled her to him. She melted against him, limp, defeated, her body shaking with great, wracking sobs. Knotting her fists in his shirt, she buried her wet face against his chest and wept, drifted into a dulled consciousness, then roused to weep again.

Time stopped. How long they clung to each other neither knew nor cared. Darkness deepened. Thin clouds drifted across the moon and filtered its light, shrouding the creek bank in eerie blackness, matching Mary's mood.

A million questions she had smothered with her grief

screamed for an answer, but were summed up in only one.

"How long?"

"Six months, maybe less. But we can live a lifetime in whatever time I have left. I got a lot to do, Mary. I'll be leaving day after tomorrow."

"Leaving? I don't understand. Where are you going?"

"New Mexico. I've got to make some fast money. Bounty hunting is the fastest way I know. There's two brothers that killed a family over in Arizona. There's a bounty on them, dead or alive. I'm going after them. I aim to collect that bounty."

"But, no, T. J., please don't go. You could be killed," Mary begged in a small, strained voice.

"It's settled, Mary. I'll be leaving at first light, day after tomorrow."

She covered her face with both hands to smother a sob but knew in her heart that it would be useless to argue further. The decision had been made and that was the end of it.

"The children, they have a right to know," she conjured up the courage to say.

"I'll talk to them tomorrow."

It was still in the deepest part of the night when T. J. slipped quietly out of bed, pulled on his pants, picked up his boots, and slipped noiselessly out the door. Outside, he sat down on the edge of the porch and stomped into his boots before strolling down to the corral.

The buckskin snorted, tossed its big head, and trotted over to the fence to meet its new master. Reaching through the wooden rails T. J. scratched the gelding's neck and ears and spoke to the horse as if it were a good friend.

"Looks like you and me got some miles to cover, big fellow. No doubt you're up to it, I just hope I am."

He hated to leave. He would much rather spend whatever time he had left right here with Mary and the kids, but he had to think of their future without him. Neither of them had family they could go to for help. They simply couldn't make it without money to help them get by. He felt he had no other choice.

His biggest worry right now was how to tell the kids. How would they take it? Could he make them understand? He had never been much on words, let alone trying to explain something even he didn't understand.

Dawn broke slowly. Darkness was pushed aside by a gradual graying of the eastern sky. Heavy clouds drifted in from the west. They were about to get some much needed rain.

Turning, he trudged slowly to the house. The lamp was lit and a thin wisp of smoke trailed skyward from the chimney. Mary was up making coffee. He paused long enough to gather an armload of wood from the stack against the side of the cabin, then pushed through the door.

Mary swung a gaze. Their eyes met. Her lips quivered. Her eyes were red. T. J. piled his armload of firewood in the woodbox and walking over, took his wife in his arms. For a long time he held her. His heart hurt with each jerk of her body as she sobbed silently.

"What's wrong, Mother?" Marilyn asked as she entered the room, brushing her long, golden hair. "Why are you crying?"

"It's...your father is going on a trip. I'll explain it to you later."

His oldest daughter's eyebrows questioned the explanation, but she said nothing further, she just set about helping her mother start breakfast. T. J. poured himself a mug of steaming coffee and settled into a chair at the table. Taking a sip, he felt the pleasant burn of the hot liquid against his lips.

"Looks like rain today," he commented, anxious to change the subject. "Me and Tad need to get that wheel fixed and back on that work wagon. Is your brother up yet?"

"I shook him awake," Marilyn said, "but he probably just turned over and went back to sleep like he usually does."

Without comment, T. J. set down his mug, pushed from his chair, and headed for the lean-to room that served as a bedroom for all three children. He had meant to add another larger room to the cabin in the spring, but now...

Tad lay curled up on his small cot, sleeping soundly. For a long minute T. J. stared down at his son, soon to be the man of the house. The boy's black, collar-length hair tumbled in usual disarray. His brown, weathered skin was still soft like new leather. The slightest hint of peach fuzz was starting to show on his upper lip. A huge lump swelled in T. J.'s throat and threatened to choke him.

"Time to get up, boy. We got a lot of work to do today. The chores need tending to."

Tad's dark eyes slammed open and went wide. Throwing back the covers and grabbing his britches, he pulled them on quickly.

"I'm sorry, Pa. I musta overslept. It won't happen again."

"A man that ain't up and about by daylight never will amount to much. Remember that, son."

"Yes, sir."

Breakfast consisted of biscuits and thick gravy, with fresh milk to drink. As one of his usual chores, Tad had hurriedly milked the cow while the womenfolk fixed breakfast.

"Today's wash day," Mary commented to her daughter during breakfast, "but your father says it looks like rain, so we'll put it off a day or two until it clears up. But there's mending to do, and Sally, don't forget to feed the chickens and gather the eggs right after breakfast, you hear me?"

"Yes, Ma'am," Sally said around a mouthful of food.

"And don't talk with your mouth full."

T. J. saw the quick looks that were exchanged between Marilyn and Tad, looks that said they knew something was wrong but didn't know what.

"Shore a good breakfast," T. J. said, draining the last sip of coffee from his mug. "Come on, son. Time's awastin'. That wagon wheel ain't gonna fix itself."

The air was hot and stale in the barn and both father and son were drenched with sweat. T. J. blotted his brow with the back of an arm and surveyed their mornings work. The broken wheel was repaired and back in place on their old wagon. They seldom used it since they'd bought the Great Northern last year. Now it would have to serve as their only transportation.

"Grease up that wheel real good, son. If a wheel goes dry it will wear out real quick, remember that."

"Yes sir."

"Now that I sold our best team of horses, you'll have to use the team of work mules if your mother has to go into town for any reason."

"Where you going, Pa? You're talking like you won't be here."

Here it is, T. J. thought. *The time I've been dreading is here. This is one of the hardest things I've ever had to do. I'd rather take a whipping than do what I got to do, but it falls on me to do it.*

"Sit down, son. We got some man-to-man talking to do."

T. J. sat down on a log and Tad pulled up the milking stool. Glancing at his son, T. J. saw a worried expression crawling across his son's face. Swallowing hard, he began.

"Son, there's some things going on that I got to tell you about and there just ain't no easy way to say it. When I went into town, it wasn't just to get supplies. I went to see the doctor. I've got something inside me that's eating my insides. The doctor says there ain't no cure for it."

Confusion, fear, the edge of panic, T. J. saw all these emotions etched on Tad's young face. It was clear his son was struggling hard not to cry. He stared at the ground, biting his lower lip, swiping at his damp eyes with a sleeve.

"Does that mean...are you fixing to die, pa?" he asked, looking up at his father with searching, tear stained eyes, his voice quivering.

A single nod of his father's head caused Tad to catch a shaky breath and again drop his head, shaking it from side-to-side. A huge sob burst from deep in his chest. His young body shook uncontrollably. T. J. gathered the boy in his arms. Tad wept a good long time. T. J. held his son until the boy cried himself out.

"It ain't fair, pa." Tad pleaded, "It ain't fair."

"I'm sorry, son. I wish I could make things different, but that's the way of it sometimes. Life ain't always fair."

"I'll be riding out before first light tomorrow. There's two outlaws down in New Mexico with bounty on their heads. Your mother will need all the money I can scrape together just to get by.

"Tad, you're already more man than most men I know. You can already ride and shoot and hunt with the best of them. When I'm gone you'll be the man of the house. I'm depending on you, son. It will fall on you to look out for your mother and sisters. I know that's putting a mighty big load square on your shoulders. But a man's got to do what a man's got to do."

"I ought to be back before hog killin' time. If something happens and I don't make it back, don't come looking or nothin' like that, just look after things here that's got to be done. Butcher that barrow with the white spot behind his ear. The meat will have to be cured out real quick, especially if the weather don't cool down after the first frost."

T. J. rose and walked over to the feed bin and from behind a stack of sacks, pulled out a long object wrapped in a cloth and handed it to his son.

"Reckon every man needs his own rifle."

Surprise and disbelief washed over Tad's face as he swiped away tears with the back of a hand and slowly unwrapped the gift. Withdrawing the shiny new Henry repeating rifle, Tad caressed it, running a hand over the polished stock. Working the lever, he checked to insure it was unloaded, then raised it to his shoulder and sighted down the barrel.

"Pa, it's the most beautiful rifle in the whole wide world. Is it really all mine?"

"It's yours, son. See you take care of it and it'll last you a lifetime."

"Thanks, Pa. Thank you so much. I'll shore take care of it don't you worry about that."

Side-by-side father and son walked to the house to let him show off his new rifle. Reaching a hand, T. J. circled his son's shoulders with an arm. *Feels good,* he thought.

They made love that night. Nestled in the soft, sweet smelling hayloft over the barn, a place they often visited, they made love, slow and honey-sweet. For a short time, Mary put out of her mind her husband's terminal condition. For fleeting moments she tried to forget that with the coming of dawn he would be leaving, perhaps for the last time. For now, just for now, he was here beside her. That wasn't enough, not nearly enough, but it was all she had.

Raising her head, she stared into her husband's eyes and saw her own yearning mirrored there. His fingers rose to brush along her cheek, to pluck a straw from her hair, to slide down the long, graceful curve of her throat.

"You're everything I ever wanted and more than I ever hoped

to have," he whispered in his wheezy voice. "You're the best thing that ever happened to me."

Mary closed her eyes and cuddled closer, losing herself in the indescribable rapture of his nearness. She felt her cheeks flush and a breath of cool air brushed against her bare skin. Even after all these years she still felt the same excitement, the same expectation as she had that very first time. He kissed her with a sweet, simmering intensity that set her head spinning and sent delight surging through her entire being. Then they made love again.

It was raining. Overnight the skies had grown dark and heavy. The thirsty ground drank patiently in the gray dawn. The first light of day struggled to push aside the darkness. The pack mule stood loaded with his trail supplies and the saddled buckskin pawed anxiously at the ground.

Even with his long rain slicker on, T. J. shivered at the chilly September morning. Standing over to one side, Mary held Sally in her arms. His daughter's head was buried in her mother's shoulder. Marilyn stood beside her mother, staring at the ground, weeping softly. Tad stood apart, scraping a line in the dirt floor with the toe of his shoe.

"So long, son," T. J. said around the knot in his throat and reaching to grasp his son's hand in a warm handshake. "Remember, I'm depending on you."

"I'll remember, Pa," the man-child said through quivering lips. His voice frayed and tears broke free. "I won't let you down."

T. J. turned his gaze to his oldest daughter. One look and she rushed into his open arms, sobbing uncontrollably.

"I love you so much, Papa," she choked out.

"I love you too, baby. Always be the best you can be, remember that."

After a long minute he reluctantly loosed himself from his daughter's embrace. Reaching, he took Sally from her mother and wrapped her in his arms. *If only I could stop time,* he thought, *and make this moment last forever.*

"You be a big girl now," he told his pouting daughter. "And mind your Ma."

She clung to him as he handed her to her older sister, refusing to let go. Pressing his lips to her cheek he pulled her back to him in a final hug. He felt his eyes mist. A lump formed in his throat and his vision blurred as he blinked back tears.

His gaze swung to his wife. Tears flowed freely from her blue eyes and coursed down her cheeks. Both hands were knotted in her dress as if she was afraid to let go. Extending both arms, he invited her into them with a single nod of his head. Two running steps and she filled them with her presence.

Their gazes sought and found each other. Their lips breached the slight distance between them and they kissed with a long, slow intensity as if trying to store up enough of the moment to last the rest of their lives.

Finally the moment ended. Without a word T. J. turned, pulled his black, wide brimmed hat lower, and threading a stirrup with his boot, swung into the saddle. As he kneed the buckskin forward Sally's small voice called out through choking sobs from behind him.

"Please don't go, Papa. Please don't go!"

He didn't dare look back. They would have seen the tears pouring from his squinted eyes.

CHAPTER III

T he time was noon. The boiling sun bore down relentlessly and cooked the white sand oven hot. Lupe Ramirez could feel the heat burning through his callused bare feet as he stepped into the single, sandy street and hurried toward the saloon.

As usual this time of day, Alamogordo, New Mexico Territory looked deserted. Most of the town's hundred or so residents were holed up in a shade somewhere wiping sweat and wishing they were someplace else.

That's what Lupe would be doing, too, if he didn't have to fetch a bottle for Mr. Giddons. Lupe accepted his role as the town's *"go fer."* He had managed to survive all of his fifteen years on the meager handouts and the few odd jobs he was able to get around town. B*ut what else could he do?* he thought, he didn't know anything else.

Lupe clutched his tattered sombrero and ducked his head as a howling westerly wind whipped up a cloud of sand and sent it racing between the adobe buildings on either side of the narrow street. The sand stung his face like a thousand hot needles.

Midway across the street something made him pause. A strange feeling swept over him. Lupe recognized the feeling; it was the feeling of death. He had been within a hair's-breath of death many times in the fifteen short years of his life. Squinting through narrowed eyes against the blowing sand, his gaze moved toward the west. What he saw sent shivers of fear racing through him. A rider on a pale horse with a pack mule following closely seemed to float out of the shimmering heat waves and was coming straight toward him.

The rider seemed to be a tall man, but rode slumped in the saddle. A gust of wind fluttered the long canvas duster about his legs. A black, flat brimmed hat partially hid a gaunt face fixed straight ahead, but the dark eyes darted like a cat from side to side, staring at nothing, seeing everything. A double barreled, sawed-off shotgun lay across his lap, held there by a gloved hand.

Lupe wanted to run, to hide, to somehow escape the overwhelming feeling of fear that twisted his insides. Instead, he stood motionless, frozen in his tracks, yet afraid to look, lest the rider was coming for him. He risked a quick glance through lowered eyes at the rider's face. And saw the face of death.

The rider reined up directly in front of Lupe. His face was ugly, his eyes piercing and fixed on Lupe.

"Where's the law?" the stranger said in a gravelly, whispered voice.

Lupe swallowed hard and still couldn't make sound come from his quivering lips. Instead, he raised a hand and pointed. Without another word the little procession moved past, then up the street toward the town marshal's office.

Tom Short jerked awake. He blinked his eyes open and sat upright on the little rawhide-bottom bunk, then tried to focus his eyes on the man standing in the open front door. The bright light from outside framed the man's silhouette and hid his features.

"You the law?" The intruder asked with a whispered voice.

"Marshal Tom Short, and who might you be?" The marshal asked, resentment clearly evident in his voice at having his *siesta* interrupted.

"Name's Littlejohn, T. J. Littlejohn. From the south plains of Texas, near Lubbock," the tall stranger said, taking a couple of steps forward and pitching a wanted poster into the marshal's lap. "You know them two?"

He glanced at the flier, then quickly up at the face of the man before him. For a long minute he stared. He decided he had never seen such an ugly hombre. "Yeah, I know them. That's the Sanchez brothers. What about it?"

"I hear they growed up hereabouts."

"Yeah, so did a lot of folks. You a bounty hunter, Mister?"

"It's a living."

"Not to my way of thinking it ain't. Nothing but hired killers, I say. No better than the ones you hunt down."

The remark awakened T. J.'s bad temper. When he spoke again the words came out cold and hard, like hot nuggets from the business end of the bone handled Colt he wore tied low on his right hip.

"Easy there, mister. That tin star you got pinned on your shirt don't mean spit to me. I've come a long ways and I'm tired and don't have much time. You're supposed to be the law around here."

"This *tin star* says *town marshal*. What happens outside town ain't none of my affair. The Sanchez boys growed up here and they got lots of kin and friends in these parts. I know them, but I don't know you."

"So it don't matter to you they made the father watch while they raped his wife and two daughters up near Tucson, then cut their throats?"

"Nobody's proved to me they done that."

"So that's the way it is?" T. J. said through clenched teeth.

"That's the way it is."

"I'll find them, Marshal, with or without your help. I'm not a man who gives up easy. It's just a matter of time."

Without another word Littlejohn turned on his heel and stalked out the door. As he climbed into the saddle he saw the young Mexican standing in front of the saloon. The boy reminded him of his son back home, about the same age.

Reining his horse over, he leaned forward in the saddle and examined the boy closer. *Dirty, tattered clothes, skinny as a rail, obviously dirt-poor, looks hungry as all get out.* T. J. felt sorry for the boy.

"I'm looking for the Sanchez brothers, son. You know 'em?"

T. J. saw fear wash across the boy's face. His gaze darted from side to side, as if searching to make sure no one overheard the question before vigorously shaking his head, then spinning around, he disappeared into the saloon.

Not a bad idea, T. J. thought. He'd always heard it said that in every town in the West there were two places to get information, the saloon and the livery. *Guess I'll try both.*

He'd already decided on a plan he hoped would flush the Sanchez brothers out of their hiding place. He knew searching for them on his own would take a lot of valuable time—something he didn't have. Instead, his plan was to ask a lot of questions, deliberately stir up things, let it be known that he was a bounty hunter and that he was on their trail...Goad them into coming after *him* to protect their reputation as *tough guys.* Just maybe they would do part of his job for him.

To be sure, he was taking a big chance. They might decide to hightail it out of the country. Doing it this way was completely against his nature. It also made the job much more dangerous, but otherwise, he could spend his whole six months chasing them all over New Mexico and still end up facing them on *their* terms, when *they* decided. No, this was his only chance. He had to take it for Mary and the kids.

Stepping down from his horse, a sharp pain suddenly hit him in the pit of his stomach and doubled him over. Grimacing, he grabbed hold of his saddle horn to keep from falling. It felt like the point of a knife piercing his insides. *Is this the start of it?* He wondered.

Gritting his teeth, he clung to the saddle with one hand and to his stomach with the other. Beads of sweat dripped from his forehead. He swallowed hard to keep from vomiting. He thought of the bottle of laudanum in his saddlebags. *Wonder if I ought to take some?* He decided to wait. It took a few minutes before the pain subsided.

Wiping sweat from his face with the back of a hand, he stripped off his gloves and used them to slap trail dust off his sleeves before jamming them down under his belt. He shucked out of his long duster and tied it behind his saddle. He thumbed the traveling loop from the hammer of his Colt and checked the load in his shotgun that hung by a rawhide loop from his left wrist. *Man can't be too careful,* he thought, *especially in my newly adopted profession.*

The saloon was an adobe structure. The only opening to the street was an open door with two batwings on it. He stopped before entering and let his gaze do a slow sweep of the room.

One room with a doorway in back, covered by a blanket. Long bar along left side.

Bartender in dirty apron behind bar handing bottle to the young Mexican boy. Several tables, two occupied. One with two Mexicans, three local types at the other.

He pushed inside. He could feel every eye in the room fix on him as he entered and strode casually to the bar with a slow, long-legged gait.

"Whiskey," he said in a raspy, hoarse whisper, laying the shotgun on the bar in front of him.

The barman was a thick set, hulk of a man with a barrel chest man and a week's growth of brown stubble on his face and a balding head. He eyed both T. J. and the scattergun suspiciously as he poured the drink. "Stranger in town, ain't ye?"

"Reckon you could say that."

"Looking fer work or jest passing through?"

"I'm looking for a couple of fellows who live around these parts, the Sanchez brothers. Ever hear of 'em?"

"Who ain't?"

"Know where I might find 'em?"

"Nope. Wouldn't tell you if I did."

Turning around, he raised his voice so all the customers could hear. "I'm looking for the Sanchez brothers. If any of you gents know where I could find them, I'll be over at the hotel for a couple of days. I'll make it worth your while."

The customers just looked away, saying nothing.

"Don't count on it, friend," the bartender said. "Talking too much ain't real healthy around here."

"I'll find 'em. It's just a matter of time."

The young Mexican turned to leave with the bottle. As he passed his dark eyes cut a quick glance and made eye contact. T. J. thought he read a look of warning in them

He could hear the buzz of whispers and feel stares burning holes in his back as he finished his drink and left the bar.

Outside, he swept the street with a searching gaze before toeing a stirrup and swinging his buckskin toward the General Store.

Down the street in front of the hotel, a little knot of people formed. They were watching three mounted cowboys as they harassed the young Mexican boy who'd just left the bar.

They had him circled in the middle of the street. They reined their horses to bump him back and forth. When he tried to escape between them they used coiled lariat ropes to whip him back into the circle. The youngest looking rider swung his rope and knocked the boy to the ground. The boy rolled and scrambled to avoid being stepped on by the horses' plunging hooves or get hit again by the heavy swinging ropes.

T. J. stared at the hazing and began to work up a mad. It was a cruel display of inhumanity. His heart screamed out for him to intervene, but his head told him otherwise. *I'm here to find the Sanchez brothers. If I get involved in this business it'll most likely end in a fight, or worse. The odds are three to one. I could get killed or kill one of them and end up in prison, or hung. Then I sure enough couldn't help my family. No. I can't take the chance.*

Turning his buckskin he forced himself to look away and headed for the store. Stepping down and looping the buckskin's reins over a hitching rail he climbed the steps to the boardwalk in front of the store. Wooden barrels sat along the front of the store and held all kinds of shovels, hoes, and ax handles. A big, bald fellow with a dirty apron tied around his middle was loading sacks of feed onto a wagon backed up to a loading platform at the side of the store. A little bell rang as T. J. pushed open the door.

Walls of the single room store were lined with floor-to-ceiling shelves stocked with everything one could imagine. Racks held clothes of all kinds for both men and women. Tables were piled high with all kinds of merchandise. There was even a stack of pine coffins stacked along the back wall. *This man is a busy fellow,* he thought as he browsed around.

"How can I help you?" The big fellow asked as he came through the back door, moping sweat from his face with the dirty apron.

"I need a box of twelve-gauge, double-aught buckshot shells."

"For that?" The storekeeper asked, pointing a look at the shotgun dangling from T. J.'s wrist. "That's a scary looking thing."

"Looking for the Sanchez brothers. Know where I could find them?"

"Yeah, I already heard there was a bounty hunter in town."

"News travels fast."

"More than you know. Watch your backside," the man said, pushing the box of shells across the counter.

"Thanks for the advice, friend, I'll do that," T. J. said, laying the money on the counter and scooping up the box.

The ruckus in front of the hotel had broken up when he came out of the store. He couldn't help feeling bad about not helping the Mexican boy and wondered if he was hurt bad.

A small wind kicked up a scattering of dust devils as he headed for the livery stable. The old Mexican liveryman was a friendly sort of fellow. A smile that occupied most of his wrinkled face greeted T. J. as he rode through the doublewide doors of the adobe building and climbed down.

"*Buenas Noches, señor.* You wish to stable and feed your horse and pack mule? Fifty cents each."

Looking past the liveryman, T. J. spotted the young Mexican boy cleaning out a stall with a shovel. Even from where he was, he could see an ugly red welt along one side of his face where the lariat rope had struck him. His nose was bleeding too.

"Yeah, double grain 'em both and put 'em in a stall, they've come a ways. The boy work for you?"

"Lupe?" The old fellow asked, twisting a look over his shoulder. "*Ah, Si,* he is a good boy, very hardworking. Some of Buck Slade's men are always picking on him though. He has no home. He sleeps in the shack out back."

"Is he okay? Where's his folks?"

"They have done worse to him before. His mother died when he was just a little pup. Don't know who his father was."

"Too bad. Can't help feeling sorry for him."

"Yeah, it's a shame the way some folks treat him."

"I'm looking for the Sanchez brothers. Don't reckon you could tell me where I might find them?"

"Could, but won't. Them two are poison mean. Can't afford to get on their bad side."

"I understand. Thanks anyway, old timer." T. J. said, as he withdrew his Henry Rifle from the saddle boot and handed the liveryman a dollar. "I'll be staying over at the hotel for a few days."

"Watch yourself," the old fellow said.

The Trails End Hotel, as the faded sign indicated, was aptly named, T. J. figured as he approached the building. It was a two-story boxy structure of weathered, unpainted planks. A small balcony along the front overlooked the street. A set of steps clung to the side and led to the second floor. Stepping through the door, he found himself in a small lobby occupied by two worn out stuffed chairs and a counter. A stairway led to the second floor.

"Afternoon," the red-faced, heavy-set fellow behind the counter said.

"Afternoon, got an empty room?"

"Got eight rooms. Four down. Four up. All empty except number one downstairs. That's my room. What's your pleasure?"

"How much?"

"Dollar a night."

"Give me one upstairs overlooking the street." T. J. said, laying a half-eagle on the counter.

"That'd be room number six," the man said, scooting the key across the counter.

"Where could a hungry fellow get a decent meal?"

"That'd be Sadie's place. Far end of the street on the right, just past the General Store."

"Think I'll mosey up and eat a bite."

T. J. could feel folks eyeing him as he strode up the boardwalk. Those coming toward him suddenly veered across the street to avoid coming face-to-face. It wasn't a good feeling.

Sadie's café was small, but surprisingly clean and neat. Red and white checkered oilcloth covered the four tables, two of which were occupied. Two men sat at one, Marshal Short sat alone at the other. T. J. chose the one nearest the back.

Scraping out a chair he folded into it as a large woman with flaming red hair pulled back in a bun shuffled up and poured him a cup of steaming coffee.

"Got beef stew for supper tonight," she said, lifting a crooked smile from one corner of her thick lips.

"Sounds good to me," he told her.

The two men at the nearby table were sneaking glances and whispering to one another as T.J. lifted his cup and blew away the steam.

"You find those fellows you been looking for?" The marshal asked sarcastically.

"Not yet, but I'm getting closer. Like I said, just a matter of time."

The words barely got out when one of his coughing spells hit him. The deep, wracking cough shook his body, doubling him over. Shoving back quickly from the table he headed for the door. He didn't make it in time. Blood spewed between the fingers of his hand that tried to cover his mouth and dripped a trail to the door.

Ducking around the corner of the building he fell to his knees, emptying his stomach of the dark red life-blood again and again. Finally it stopped. He rose stooped, and staggered on weak legs to the nearby watering trough to wash his face in the lukewarm water.

Sensing a presence, he twisted a look behind him. Marshal Short stood, leaning against the front of the café.

"Seems to me like you got worse problems than the Sanchez boys," he said. "Anything I can do?"

T. J. stared at him for a minute with a puzzled look as he wiped his face on a shirtsleeve, then offered a single shake of his head. "But thanks anyway."

The Marshal turned and headed down the street. A few steps away he paused as though he might turn back then headed on toward his office.

Reckon I'll pass on the beef stew tonight, T. J. decided.

T. J.'s stomach still wasn't settled as he stood at the open window of room number six and pushed the faded, dirty curtain aside with the back of a curled finger. The room was bare except for an iron-post bed, and a small dresser with a water pitcher and basin. The bed was little more than a cot. The worn, corn shuck mattress was so thin it would have made a dandy blanket on cold nights. Rooms five and six looked out over the balcony down into the deserted street. A narrow hallway divided rooms five and six from seven and eight, which were on the backside of the hotel. A stairway at one end of the open hallway led down into the lobby. A door in the other end opened to the outside steps leading down to the street.

Off to the west, the evening sun gently kissed the horizon. As he watched, the golden-red ball shot streaks of red, gold, orange, and yellow across the blue sky and set the white clouds ablaze with flaming color. T. J. loved to watch the sunsets; they were never the same. *Reckon how many sunsets I got left?* He was embarrassed by the coughing spell in the café. It was the first one he'd had since he left home a week before, but they were getting more frequent and severe.

With the setting of sun, dusk came quickly. Racing silently across the desert countryside, it swallowed up the light. As he watched, dark settled in.

Down in the street, a few stragglers hurried home, most likely to a waiting supper. *Mary and the kids would be sitting down to the supper table about now. Wish I was there,* he thought, feeling that familiar ache in his heart. *But I've got a job to do.*

With that thought he turned away from the window quickly and double-checked his weapons, making sure they were all fully loaded. Satisfied, he laid down on the bed to wait. *Will the Sanchez brothers come tonight?*

CHAPTER IV

Mary Littlejohn stared down at the plateful of food in front of her and picked at it; she hadn't had an appetite since her husband left. The children sat on benches on either side. T. J.'s place, at the head of the table, sat conspicuously empty.

For a solid week—Sunday to Sunday—she hadn't felt like doing anything. It was as if her whole world had ended when she watched T. J. ride away. *How can I go on without him?* She asked herself for the thousandth time. *I'm not strong enough, or wise enough, or brave enough. What if I fail? What will we do? What will happen to us?* Those and a million other questions that she smothered in her grief and drowned with her tears whirled through her mind.

For eighteen years he had been her rock, her strength. Eighteen wonderful years. Her mind flicked back to the first time she laid eyes on him.

It was a Sunday, just like today. It was my sixteenth birthday. I was coming out of the Methodist Church where my father was the pastor. I had on that light blue dress and my blue bonnet with the white lace around it. Elaine, my best friend, and I were planning a picnic down by the creek that afternoon to celebrate my birthday. I looked up and there he was.

I still remember how my heart almost leaped right out of my chest. He was so handsome: tall, dark and handsome, every girl's dream. He was riding down the road in front of the church. His long, black hair hung well below the collar of his buckskin shirt.

I remember how he looked at me, how our eyes met and held for what seemed like an eternity, and somehow I knew without a doubt this was the man I wanted to spend the rest of my life with.

Elaine thought I was crazy when I leaned over and whispered to her, "That's the man I'm going to marry." She took one look at him, giggled, and said, "Oh, he's ugly." I never really liked her much after that.

How he knew about the picnic I still don't know, but he rode up, and we talked, and, against the objections of both of my parents, were married a month later.

Hard times?—oh yes! For the preacher's daughter to marry a half-breed was the end of the world to hear my parents tell it. We were caught in a No Man's Land between two cultures. Former friends shunned me, even my parents practically disowned me, but oh, I was in heaven on earth. Then, barely two months after we were married, he brought me here to our valley.

Absently, Mary lifted her coffee mug and sipped the strong liquid, hoping to quell the churning nausea in her stomach. *I've got to snap out of it,* she told herself. *We can't just stop living. There's work to be done. T. J. is depending on me. I've got to be strong for the children, and for him.*

"Children, I want to apologize to you. I've let you down. For the last week I have moped around, feeling sorry for myself. I've let the work around here go undone and haven't shouldered my share. Tad, if you hadn't kept up with the chores I don't know what we would have done. Like your father said, you're more man than most men. Marilyn, you have done most of the cooking and cleaning and I thank you. You are quite a young lady.

"Yes, we are facing some hard times. I don't know how we will make it, but we will make it. Life is hard, and sometimes isn't fair, but every moment of it is a precious gift from God and I'm ashamed I've wasted this past week.

"From this moment on this family is going to hold our heads up, stand together, and face whatever comes against us. Now let's join hands and thank the Lord for his blessings. I'll begin."

Joining hands, they all bowed their heads and closed their eyes.

"Dear God," Mary said softly. "I thank you for your bounty. You have blessed us in so many ways. Forgive me for questioning you. I still don't understand it, and I beg for more faith to deal with my lack of understanding. Give me the strength I need. Wherever T. J. is tonight, I pray you watch over him and protect him, and help him know in his heart of hearts that we love him. Amen"

For a long moment silence filled the room. Only the soft crackling of the fire interrupted the reverence of the moment.

"God," Tad finally said, "bless Ma and Pa and Sis and Little-Bit, and help me not to let Pa down. Amen"

"Our Heavenly Father," Marilyn prayed. "I ask that you be with my father tonight wherever he is. Bless Mother, and Tad and Sally. Amen."

There was no hesitation when it Sally's turn came.

"And, God, help Pa catch those bad old men. Amen!"

Later, lying alone in her bed, Mary muffled her sobs with the edge of a quilt lest the children hear. Tears drizzled hot between her fingers. Her heart ached. She knotted her fists in the bedclothes and buried her wet face in the covering. *Oh, T. J. I miss you so. You should have never promised me "always." Life is too fragile, too uncertain.*

The first hint of dawn slanted in through the open window and colored the darkness of T.J.'s little room. Somewhere, a rooster announced another day. *Another day,* T. J. thought.

It had been a restless, sleepless night. He'd dozed off a few times, only to snap wide awake at the slightest sound. Tired of the bed, he rose, stomped on his boots, and washed his face in the wash pan on the little bench in the corner.

Turning left in the hallway, he pushed through the door to the outside steps and went down to the street. Alamogordo was starting to come awake. A stray dog trotted down the dusty street. Several roosters joined the chorus and carried out their morning ritual. Up the street, the storekeeper swept the boardwalk. T. J. headed that way.

"Morning," the man greeted cheerfully, stopping his chore and leaning on his broom as T. J. drew near.

"Morning."

"You're up and about mighty early."

"Thought I'd see if Miss Sadie's got the coffee pot on."

"Oh, it's on and hot. I've already smelled the bacon frying."

"Think I'll see if I can get around some breakfast, kinda tired eating my own cooking."

"Never did catch your name yesterday?"

"Name's Littlejohn, T. J. Littlejohn, from over near Lubbock, Texas on the south plains. He said, sticking out a hand.

"Ben Higgins," the storekeeper said, taking the offered hand and shaking it firmly. "Planning on staying in town long?"

"Till I get the Sanchez boys. Ain't leaving till I do."

"Wish I could help you, Mr. Littlejohn, but I got a wife and two youngins. Them brothers are a spiteful pair, no telling what they'd do if they found out I helped you. I just can't take the chance."

"They ever cause trouble around here?"

"They've been in and out of trouble most of their life, just little stuff mostly, nothing bad serious. Some think they was the ones that robbed and killed a traveling drummer awhile back. Somebody shot him in the back and stole a bunch of cash I'd just paid him for a load of supplies. Nothing ever come of it though. The marshal never could find any proof.

"What's got most folks scared is what they're supposed to have done over in Arizona. That's bad business, raping those folks and cutting their throats."

"They ever come into town?"

"Oh, you bet. Free as you please. They've got a lot of kin in these parts."

"Reckon by now they know I'm looking for them."

"You can bet on it. They know all right. I'd shore watch my backside if I was you."

"Intend to. Good day to you, Mr. Higgins."

"You take care, Mr. Littlejohn."

Sadie looked up from wiping a table as T. J. entered. He touched a thumb and finger to the brim of his hat.

"Miss Sadie, I'm sure sorry for getting sick in here last night. I feel awfully bad about it. Wondering if I was still welcome?"

"Sure couldn't have been anything you ate of mine," she chuckled, motioning to a chair. "You lit out before you ate. Course you're welcome. Have a seat and I'll pour you some coffee."

"I'm obliged. If my nose is telling me the truth, some of that bacon and about three eggs shore would go down good."

"Won't take but a minute, how you like 'em?"

"Still runny."

She filled a cup with steaming coffee and headed for the kitchen. "You're the bounty hunter everybody's talking about ain't you?"

"Reckon so."

"Looking for the Sanchez brothers, I hear," she hollered from the kitchen.

"Yep. Know where I could find 'em?"

"Knowing them boys, I reckon if you just sit still long enough they'll find you."

"Kind of the way I had it figured, to. What's their names, the Sanchez boys I mean?"

"Juan and Jose. They're mean, bad mean. But Jose is the worst. You're a sick man ain't you, Mr. Littlejohn?"

"I've been better."

"I've got you pegged as a married man too. Am I right?"

"Yep."

"Children too, I figure?"

"Yep."

"Thought so. You look the kind. I can usually tell."

T. J. sipped his coffee, feeling the pleasant burn against his lips, and thought about what she had said. *How could she tell I was married and had kids at home?* He drained his coffee cup and poured himself another from the pot she had left on the table. He was halfway to the bottom of the second cup when she set a plateful of eggs and bacon and a pan of hot biscuits in front of him.

"None of my business," she said, pouring herself a cup and pulling out a chair. "You ever hunt bounty before?"

"First time for everything," he told her, lifting a forkful of food to his mouth.

"Figured as much. Way I got it figured, you got something bad wrong with you and you're hunting bounty to leave for your family after you're gone."

"You asking or telling?"

"Just call it a woman's intuition."

The front door opened and Marshal Short strode in and walked over to T. J.'s table.

"Morning, Sadie. Morning, Littlejohn. You feeling better?"

"Morning, Marshal. Yeah, I'm doing well. Have a seat."

"Don't mind if I do. Sadie, bring me a plateful of what he's got."

She poured both of them some more coffee and headed for the kitchen. Marshal Short peered at T. J. over the rim of his coffee cup for a long minute.

"You're shore causing a lot of talk around town," he finally said.

"Folks gotta have something to talk about, might as well be me, I reckon."

"I don't want no trouble in my town. You got trouble written all over you."

"Soon as I get what I come for, I'll be moving on. You want to get shed of me, tell me where I can find the Sanchez boys and I'll fork a saddle."

"You know I can't do that. I gotta live here."

"Then I reckon you might just as well get use to having me around."

"You're a stubborn man, Mr. Littlejohn."

"Been called that a time or two, sure enough."

Sadie brought the Marshal's breakfast and they ate in silence for a few minutes. Several other customers straggled in, spoke to the marshal, and eyed T. J. with suspicion. He finished his breakfast, drained his coffee cup, and pushed from the chair.

"Guess I'll go ask around some more," he said, clamping his hat in place. "Maybe somebody's had a change of heart."

"Don't count on it," Marshal Short said, watching T. J. as he dropped money on the table and walked out.

Swinging by the hotel, he picked up his rifle and saddlebags then stopped by and paid Mr. Gibbons for his room for another two nights.

"I'll likely be back before dark," he told the man, who was busy doctoring up his coffee from the bottle Lupe had brought him. The bottle was about empty.

At the livery, he saddled the buckskin but left Samson in the stall. The old liveryman watched as T. J. cinched his saddle.

"Just so I don't ride past the Sanchez boys without knowing it, what kind of horses should I be looking for?"

"If'n I was you I'd watch out for a black and white pinto and a red sorrel with a white blaze face and stockings. Might have trouble seeing them though with you riding into the sun."

"Much obliged, old timer," T. J. said, kneeing his horse and heading east.

All day he rode, turning down every road and trail, keeping his eyes peeled for the kind of horses the liveryman described, asking questions, getting nothing except frightened looks or shaking heads. Seemed everyone was scared to death at the very mention of their names. The sun was sliding out of sight when he rode wearily back into the livery and unsaddled the buckskin.

"Don't look like you had any luck?" The old liveryman said, taking the buckskin's reins and leading him to a stall.

"Had lots of luck, all bad. Saw a lot of country though."

"Happen to see a couple of twin peaks?"

"Yeah, now that you mention it, off to the northeast a ways."

"Stream of water over there too. Nice little valley, good place for a little spread."

"Sounds like it. I'll take a ride out that way tomorrow. I'm obliged, old timer."

"For what? You didn't hear nothing from me."

"Shore didn't."

Sadie's beef stew was still good. His first taste told him that, and the second bowl was just as good as the first. The place was crowded and Sadie had little time to visit.

"You look plumb tuckered out," she told him as she stopped long enough to pour him another cup.

"Yeah, think I'll stop by for a nightcap then hit the sack. It's been a long day."

"Don't sleep too sound," she said, giving him a long, knowing look. "See you at breakfast."

"Yeah, you can count on it," he said, dropping a dollar on the table and pushing upright.

Outside, he headed toward the saloon. Several horses were tied at the hitching rail, but no pinto, no sorrel with white blaze face. He pushed through the batwing doors.

Two tables were occupied. One with two Mexicans, the other by three tough looking cowboys, the same ones he had seen the day before hazing the Mexican boy, Lupe. They eyed him suspiciously as he walked to the bar.

"Whiskey," he said in his raspy, hoarse whisper, laying the shotgun on the bar in front of him.

"You find them fellows you was looking for?" The barkeeper asked, pouring T. J.'s drink.

"Nope, not yet."

Just then Lupe hurried through the door. T. J. saw the boy glance at the three toughs, then quickened his pace to the bar.

"Mr. Sam, Mr. Gibbons wants a bottle," he told the barman.

"I swear to my time," the barkeeper complained, handing the boy a bottle. "That man can go through a bottle quicker than you can say scat."

The boy grabbed the bottle and hurried toward the door.

"Hey you, kid!" The younger man at the table hollered in a gruff voice. "Where you think you're going with *my* bottle?"

Lupe stopped dead in his tracks, swung a quick look over his shoulder at the speaker, then hurried even faster toward the door.

"Hey Kid! Get over here!" The tough hollered even louder.

T. J. turned around and leaned his back against the bar to watch what was going on. The boy stopped, turned, and walked slowly over to the table where the three toughs sat.

"Where did you think you was going with my bottle? You was trying to steal it weren't you? You ain't nothing but a thieving Mexican."

"I weren't trying to steal it. I was fetching it for Mr. Gibbons over at the hotel."

"I said you was trying to steal it! You calling me a liar?"

It was clear the boy was scared. He dropped his head and shook it back and forth.

"You ain't nothing but a boot-licking greaser!" The young bully said, lifting his half empty glass and slowly pouring it over his own boots. "Get down there and lick my boots, greaser!"

A fierce, slow-burning anger found birth in T. J.'s stomach and rippled up his spine. He felt his neck flush hot, his eyes narrow, his muscles tense. He swallowed and sucked in a deep breath.

The young, helpless boy shot frantic looks around the room, obviously searching for help and finding none. Slowly, painfully, he bent to his knees in front of the cocky young bully. Lupe hesitated for another long moment. Tears breached the corners of his eyes and coursed down his young cheeks. Then dropping to his hands and knees he lowered his head and began licking the cowboy's dirty boots. All three cowboys laughed.

"That's enough," T. J. heard himself say, his words came out as cold and chiseled as a gravestone. All three cowboys swung a look at the speaker.

"This ain't none of your affair," the young bully said loudly. "You best mind your own business, mister."

"I'm making it my business. You got no call to treat the boy that way."

Young Lupe quickly scrambled away on hands and knees.

Fixing T. J. with an angry scowl the cocky young cowboy rose and strode like a bantam rooster over to stop within an arm's length.

"Meddling in other folks business just might get you more than you can chew."

In one, lightening quick move, T. J. swept the shotgun off the bar and slammed it across the bully's nose sending blood splaying through the air. The sickening sound of bone shattering resounded across the room. The bully dropped like a sack of potatoes, out cold.

The man's two partners leaped to their feet, knocking over chairs, clawing for their pistols. T. J.'s continuous motion swung the nose of the shotgun around to cover them. The metallic double click of both hammers being pulled back in place could be heard all over the room. Both men froze in place, their pistols still halfway out of their holsters.

Without diverting his gaze from the two toughs, T. J. shifted his head slightly and spoke over his shoulder to the bartender. "What about you? You buying into this?"

"No, Sir!" the barkeeper said nervously. "I didn't lift a finger."

"Good. Keep it that way," T. J. said. "You two, one at a time, ease them hoglegs out and toss them over here on the floor, right easy like."

Being extra careful, they both did as he had ordered.

"Now pick up your partner and get him outta here. Tell him the next time I see him I'll kill him."

Scrambling, they hurried over and grabbed the unconscious man under each arm and dragged him out the door. Lupe still cowed on the floor, looking like a whipped pup.

"You can get up now, son," T. J. told him. "They're gone."

Getting quickly to his feet, the boy grabbed the bottle he came after and scampered toward the door. Pausing in front of the door he turned and fixed T. J. with a stare.

"Thanks, Mister" Then the boy spun and hurried out.

"Afraid you just bought yourself a wagonload of trouble, friend," the bartender said. "Those boys are part of Buck Slade's outfit. That boy you laid out is Billy Slade, Bucks youngest son."

"Am I supposed to know who this Buck Slade fellow is?"

"If I's you, and I'm shore glad I ain't, I'd be making it my business to find out. Slade owns the biggest spread in these parts. You don't pistol whip one of his boys and live to tell about it. You can bank on it. They'll be coming looking for you by morning."

CHAPTER V

Mary was gathering clothes off the clothesline while Marilyn started supper. Tad was busy repairing the corral where one of the mules had kicked down a couple of railings. As usual, Sally was in her swing under the big oak tree nearby. It was just short of sundown.

As it did so many times during every day, her mind drifted to T. J.. *It's been eight days now. Wonder where he is and what he's doing? He said he thought he could get there in a week or less. Let's see, then a week to get back, but what if he can't find those men right away? No telling how long he could be gone.*

Absently, she glanced up at the waning sun. That's when she saw the rider on top of the hill across the creek. He was still too far off to recognize but he was coming toward the house. Living way out here it could be anybody. T. J. always said not to take any chances. Apprehension gave birth to fear and fear to panic. A cry spiraled up her throat. Her voice shredded, high-pitched and frantic.

"Tad! Someone's coming! Get in the house! Hurry!"

Dropping her basket of clothes she ran to grab Sally from the swing and rushed toward the front door. Tad was right behind her.

"Who is it, ma? Could you tell?" he said, sounding surprisingly calm.

"They're too far away. Hurry. Get your rifle, I'll close all the shutters. We can't take a chance," she told him breathlessly.

She had closed and barred the last shutter in the bedroom when Tad hollered from the front.

"It's okay, ma. It's just Sheriff Paxton from Town. Reckon what he's doing way out here?"

The question sent an arrow piercing her heart. *What would he be doing way out here unless he, oh no, oh no!*

A hand flew to her mouth stifling a gasp as she worked frantically to remove the security bar from the front door.

"Hello the house," she heard the sheriff's voice call out just before she swung the door open.

"Afternoon, ma'am," George Paxton said, touching the brim of his hat with a thumb and curled finger. "Sorry to ride in on you folks like this. T. J. asked me to look in on you if I was out this way."

"Is he, have you heard anything from him?"

"No ma'am. I was over at Jed Holly's place. He's been missing some cows lately and after I got through over there I thought I'd just ride on over here and check on you folks."

Tad squeezed past Mary and stepped onto the porch, still carrying his new Henry rifle in both hands.

"Afternoon, Mr. Paxton," he said, sounding every bit like a man, Mary thought.

"Afternoon, Tad. That's a mighty fine looking rifle you got there. Your dad said he was gonna get you one. He said you could already shoot the tail off a jackrabbit at a hundred yards and him in a dead run."

"Ah, I can shoot I reckon, but I ain't that good."

"Land sakes, George, where's my manners?" Mary asked,

wiping her hands on her apron. "I haven't even asked you to get down and come in. Climb off your horse and sit a spell. I've got some hot coffee on the stove, will you have a cup?"

"Don't mind if I do, thank you, ma'am. Been in the saddle might near all day. Truth is, I thought I smelled coffee and it shore smelled fine," he said as he swung down and ground-hitched his gray mare.

"Marilyn," Mary said over her shoulder. "Get the sheriff a cup of coffee. Tad, set your rifle down and fetch that basket of clothes into the house for me, will you, son? Have a seat there in T. J.'s rocking chair, George."

"You folks doing all right, Mrs. Littlejohn?"

"Good as could be expected, I suppose. How are things in town? I was hoping to get to town this fall but it don't look like it now with things like they are."

"I'm shore sorry about that, Mrs. Littlejohn. I still can't hardly believe it. T. J.'s always been one of the strongest men I ever knew. Him and me has been friends a long time."

"I know you have. He's always says you're the best friend he's ever had. He says you're a fine man."

"Ah, he never was much of a judge of a man, I reckon."

"Would you stay for supper, George? Just having beans and cornbread, but there's plenty. And I baked some fried apple pies today, we'd be pleased to have you if you'd stay."

"Truth is, Mrs. Littlejohn, I was sorta hoping you'd ask. It shore smells good from where I'm sitting."

Tad finished putting the clothesbasket in the house and wandered back to the front porch.

"Mr. Paxton, sir. You say Mr. Holly's been losing cows? Reckon what it is?"

"Don't know, son. Could be anything—most likely nothing. I figure they just strayed off someplace. Maybe they'll show up in a few days."

"Supper's on," Marilyn called from the kitchen.

* * *

Three bowls later, the sheriff leaned back in the chair and rubbed his stomach. "Don't know when I've ate better beans than that, Mrs. Littlejohn. I swear I think them fried pies were the best I ever ate. And that fresh buttermilk set it off just right."

"Glad you enjoyed it, George. Beans has always been one of T. J.'s favorite meals."

"A man gets tired of his own cooking after awhile, and you can't afford to eat in the café all the time."

"How long has Alice been gone now? Two, three years?"

"It'll be three years in December. Lost her and the baby both just before Christmas. The midwife said the baby was breached."

"Yes, I remember. I'm sure sorry, George, I always liked Alice."

"She was as fine a woman as ever walked the face of the earth, I reckon. I still miss her."

"I'm sure you do."

"Think I'll mosey out to the porch and have a smoke if you don't mind, then I better be on my way."

"It's getting late. Why don't you stay the night? You can sleep in the barn. Not much but you're welcome to it. T. J. had talked about building us another bedroom in the spring but . . ."

"The barn would be just fine, Mrs. Littlejohn, I'm obliged."

George Paxton sat in the rocker. Tad sat on the porch leaning his back against the cedar support post. The womenfolk sat on the edge of the porch with little Sally in her mother's lap.

"You sure you don't mind if I smoke?"

"Not at all," Mary said.

Tad watched closely as the sheriff took out the makings. He opened a cloth bag of Gold Crown tobacco and, taking a small, thin cigarette paper from a little packet, he creased it with a finger. He tapped a line of tobacco onto the paper and used his teeth to pull the drawstring shut on the bag and slipped it back in a shirt pocket. Sticking out his tongue, he licked the edge of the paper and expertly rolled the cigarette to a perfect roundness. Striking a match on his pant leg, he put fire to the cigarette and drew a long inhale.

"I never seen anybody do that before," Tad said admiringly. "Pa don't smoke. Pa says you and him rode together when you fought the Mexicans."

"Yeah we did. We fought the Indians too. Your pa saved my life one time when we was fighting a bunch of Apache on the Upper Brazos River. I would have been a goner for shore if it hadn't been for your pa."

"Really? He never said nothing about that."

"I ain't surprised. That's the kind of man your pa is. He ain't one to go around bragging."

"Tell me about it, will you, Mr. Paxton?"

"Well, your pa and me was looking for some renegade Apache that had run off from their new reservation. The way it was told to us, there weren't but a half-dozen of them so it was no big thing. Boy was that a bunch of malarkey. When we found them there must have been two dozen or more in the bunch.

"Well, sir, we knew we was in a heap of trouble so we took off and they took off right behind us, yelling and shooting and all. One of 'em got lucky and shot my horse out from under me and I went tumbling. Like I say, I was a goner for shore. I was done making peace with my maker when I looked up and here come your pa, riding hell-bent-for-leather. He had turned around and come back to get me 'stead of saving his own hide.

"Still don't know how we made it but we did, just by the skin of our teeth. Yessiree, I wouldn't be here today if it weren't for your pa. He's one of the bravest men I've ever known."

"It's time for bed, children," Mary said, swallowing hard and standing.

"Goodnight, Mrs. Littlejohn," the sheriff said, pushing from the chair. "I'll be pulling out before first light. I'm shore obliged for your hospitality."

"If you hear anything from T. J. you'll be sure to let me know won't you?"

"Shore will, Mrs. Littlejohn, first thing."

"Goodnight then."

"Goodnight, ma'am."

Lying in his room, T. J. commenced an argument with himself. *I've gone and done it again,* he thought, as he leaned his Henry rifle against the wall by the bed. He unbuckled his gun belt and draped the holster and Colt pistol over the head of the bedstead, then pried off his boots. He was dead tired.

As if I ain't already got enough trouble trying to take the Sanchez boys, now I've got some big rancher coming for me for pistol whipping his boy.

Lying back on the shaky bed he propped one arm behind his head, drew in a large inhale of air and blew it out in disgust at himself. *Why can't I learn to just keep my mouth shut?*

He didn't regret stepping in to help the boy, he knew he had done what he had to do, but now he had another problem that threatened to mess up his whole plan. Maybe tomorrow he would find the Sanchez brothers, if they didn't find him first.

Darkness claimed the little room and the street sounds drifting in through the open window gradually died down. T. J.'s tired body screamed out for rest; he had slept little the night before. He closed his eyes and sleep wrapped its soft arms around him and drew him close.

It was the thickest part of the night when they came. A squeaky board on the outside steps was the first hint that he had company. His eyes snapped open instantly. Silently he swung his bare feet to the floor and scooped up the Stevens sawed-off shotgun from the bed beside him and thumbed back both hammers until they locked in place and slung his gun belt over his shoulder. He bunched two pillows under the thin blanket to resemble a sleeper in the bed.

Tiptoeing, he crept toward the door and pressed his ear to the thin wood. He heard the muffled sound of the outside door at the end of the hallway inching open. Soft footsteps moved inside and crept slowly along the hallway, pausing just outside the door to his room. Expecting the intruder to kick in the door and come in with guns blazing, T. J. sidestepped and pressed his back flat against the wall so that when the door opened he would be behind it.

Another sound reached his hearing, it was from outside on the balcony. A second intruder had climbed up unheard and was coming at him through the open window. They had him in a crossfire. His gut tightened and he swallowed hard in a dry throat.

He was surprised when he heard a key being inserted in the lock on the door. *How did they get the key to his room?* The key turned. The bolt withdrew. The knob twisted and the door pushed slowly inward.

The room was near pitch black. Only a dim light filtered in through the open window. His sight would be of little help, he would have to rely on his hearing and instincts to guide his actions. T. J. felt the air in his lungs go stale and thin. Slowly, silently, he drew a long breath and let it out by degrees. His muscles tensed. His senses keened. His mind was focused and controlled and compelling.

He sensed, rather than saw, the window curtain being pushed aside. Only a vague silhouette appeared outlined against the night sky as a man's form eased through the window. T. J. waited.

Anticipation boiled in his gut and rolled over him like a flood. He could smell a man's presence scant inches away in the doorway and felt the intruder moving toward the bed.

When it happened it happened all at once. As if by a prearranged signal both shooters opened up at almost the same time. The loud roll of explosions from their pistols shattered the stillness. A bouquet of red blossomed out of the darkness from the shooter standing just inside the window and lit the room with a reddish glow. Both killers were standing near the bed pumping shot after shot into the bunched-up pillows.

Then, the shooting stopped. In the eerie moment of quietness a raspy, whispered voice would be the last words either of the would-be killers would ever hear.

"Welcome to Hell, boys."

The deafening explosion of a single barrel of T. J.'s shotgun shook the thin walls of the small hotel room and bathed it in an eerie light. The blast lifting the nearest man off his feet and propelling him backward across the bed. In the afterglow of light T. J. saw the second shooter lunge for the window. He didn't make it. The second load of buckshot literally blew him through the window, across the balcony, and into the street below.

With his pistol in hand, T. J. made his way over to the dresser and fumbled in his pants pocket for a match, found the coal oil lamp, and lit it. The yellow light flooded the room. The room boiled with blue gun smoke. The acrid stench burned his nostrils and brought tears to his eyes as he walked over and gazed down at the man on the bed, or what was left of him, which wasn't much.

The blast of double-aught buckshot had struck him straight on, blowing off most of his face and leaving great holes in his chest that was soaking the bed with blood. His head dangled on a stub that was once his neck. The sight turned T. J.'s stomach and threatened to make him sick.

Loud voices down in the street drew T. J.'s attention. He holstered his pistol and laid the shotgun on the dresser. He didn't want to have a gun in his hand when the law arrived.

"Over here, Marshal!" someone down in the street shouted. "There's a dead man over here. Good Lord! There's nothing left of him!"

Heavy, running steps pounded up the stairway from the lobby. Others could be heard rushing up the outside steps and down the hallway. Marshal Tom Short burst into the room with pistol in hand, followed by a half-dozen other armed men.

"What's going on here? You all right?" the Marshal asked breathlessly.

"Yeah, I'm okay," T. J. whispered. "Know who they were?"

"It was the Sanchez boys," the old liveryman said from near the doorway. "I spotted their horses down in the alley. I'd know that pinto and sorrel anywhere."

Walking over to gaze down at the one on the bed the marshal shook his head and quickly turned his face away.

"Shore couldn't tell it by looking. His own mother wouldn't recognize him."

Ben Higgins from the store pushed through the knot of men to take a look. He also served as the town undertaker.

"If some of you boys will come help me we'll bring a couple of burying boxes from the store and carry them out that way."

"Who's gonna be responsible for cleaning up the mess in here?" The hotel man, Gibbons complained. "I'll never get all that blood cleaned up."

"Shut your trap and go have a drink," Marshal Short told him, clearly irritated. "We got two dead men and all you're worrying about is your two-bit room. Guess you ought to come over to the office with me, Littlejohn. I'll need you to tell me exactly what happened."

"A man might want to wonder how they had a key to my room," T. J. said, pinning the hotel man with a questioning look.

Gibbon's face flushed crimson red. His eyes darted from one man to the other and he began slowly shaking his head.

"What about that, Gibbons?" The Marshal asked. "How come one of them boys would have a key to Mr. Littlejohn's room?"

"How...how should I know? You saying I gave them a key?"

"Not saying nothing, yet. Best I remember though, you usually got two keys for each room," the Marshal said. "Let's go down and just take a look. If there ain't a back-up key for room number six in the slot behind the counter you're gonna have some explaining to do."

"Mr. Higgins," T. J. called after the storekeeper. "Would it put you out if I come over and talked to you a minute after the marshal gets through talking to me? I got something on my mind."

CHAPTER VI

The morning sun was fresh-born and two hours old when they came. Their coming was announced by a swirling, boiling cloud of dust that rose from the desert like a northerner, then bent westerly on a stiff breeze.

Galloping hooves thundered over the dried hardpan, rumbling like distant drums. T. J. stood at his hotel room window and watched the sight that would strike fear into the heart of any man that had a lick of sense. They swept into town like an avenging horde. The breadth of the riders stretched from boardwalk to boardwalk and four or five deep.

The leader rode well out front on a coal-black stallion. The horse tore down the middle of the dusty street with its head pulled close against its neck on a tight rein and his tail held up. It had a high stepping gait, bringing its hooves high and down fast. It was a horse one might see once in a lifetime and once a fellow had seen it would never forget it.

T. J. didn't have to wonder who the rider was. He was a big man, square shouldered and thick through the chest. He rode straight and tall in the saddle, like he was born there. His chiseled face wore a no-nonsense look, like a man use to authority. He wore a fringed leather vest and a wide brimmed Stetson set at a perfect angle on his salt and pepper hair. Looped over his saddlehorn was a coiled hangman's noose. Buck Slade had come to town.

Reaching the hotel, the leader lifted a hand and reined up sharply. The prancing black stallion back-stepped and tossed its massive head, clearly spooked by the sight before it.

Leaning upright against the hitching rail in front of the hotel stood two pine coffins. Inside the coffins were the bloody remains of *Juan* and *Julio Sanchez*.

Horses scented the smell of death and rebelled. Riders fought their mounts to maintain control. For long minutes it was pure bedlam. Hardened riders got sick to their stomachs at the sight and lost their breakfast.

"Who did this?" Buck Slade demanded in a loud voice.

Bending, T. J. stepped through the opening in the upstairs wall where the window use to be. He planted his feet wide apart on the small balcony directly above the milling mass of riders. In his hand he held two sawed-off double-barreled shotguns. All four hammers were pulled back and locked in place. The twin barrels of both guns were pointed directly at the big man on the black stallion.

"Reckon that would be me," he said, his words as cold as an outhouse in the dead of winter.

Buck Slade's head snapped upward and his gaze locked on the cold, dark eyes that stared back at him.

"You'd be the bounty hunter that pistol whipped my boy. I'm going to hang you."

"You think you brought enough help?"

"My boy's lying home half dead because of you."

"Mr. Slade, your boy's a two-bit bully that picks on little

boys and lets his papa and a small army do his fighting for him. Now before you go and do something that you can't take back, you might want to decide if you want to die looking like them boys in the boxes.

"That's what a load of double-aught buckshot can do to a man at close range. I got four loads in these scatterguns. The way you boys are bunched up, I figure I can take at least a dozen of you with me, maybe more.

"Dying is forever. Now you got to ask yourself, is a broken nose worth all that?"

"You made my boy a laughing stock!" the man shouted, waving the hangman's noose in the air. "You've got to pay for that!"

"Talkin's over." T. J. said coldly. "Either turn around and ride out of here right now, or let's start the dance. It's do or die time. You got about two heartbeats to decide."

"There's been enough killing, Buck!" the Marshal's loud voice shouted from behind the mass of riders. To back up his words he too, held a double-barreled shotgun.

Over on the left, Mr. Higgins and the old liveryman stepped from the alleyway, rifles leveled at the Slade riders. Even Lupe was there with a rifle that he had got hold of someplace.

On the right several townspeople appeared, all armed and with their guns trained on the nervous cowboys.

The big rancher swiveled his head, obviously assessing the situation and not liking what he saw, then pinned T. J. with hate-filled eyes.

"This ain't over," he snarled in a cold, shaky voice. "If it's the last thing I ever do in this life I'll see you pay for this. Nobody shames a Slade and lives to brag about it! Mark my word, Mister, I'll hunt you down and you'll pay for this! You'll all pay for this!" He shouted the last threat so the whole town could hear him. Then, raising a hand, he signaled his men to ride out.

T. J. watched them ride away with a sense of relief but something told him he hadn't seen the last of Buck Slade.

The town's citizens knotted in front of the hotel, backslapping, shaking each other's hand, and congratulating themselves on backing down the high and mighty Buck Slade.

"Never in all my born days thought I'd ever see Buck Slade take backwater," the big barkeeper from the saloon said excitedly.

"We shore showed him a thing or two," somebody said. Others nodded or voiced their agreement.

"You think he meant what he said, that we'd all pay?" another asked.

"Naw, you saw him back down. He won't do nothing," somebody bragged.

"Don't bank on it," T. J. said, walking from the hotel and joining the group. "That ain't the kind of man that forgets easy. I'm obliged for your help."

"When you get ready, come on over to the office and we'll see what we got to do to take care of that reward you got coming," Marshal Short said.

"I'll be along directly," T. J. told him. "Right now me and Lupe are gonna see if Miss Sadie can rustle us up some breakfast. I'm hungry enough to eat a full-growed cow. How's that sound, son?"

The boy's face split in a nutcracker grin that almost touched his ears. "Sounds mighty good to me, Mister Littlejohn, sir."

Side by side they headed that way.

Over a plateful of flour biscuits and thicken gravy, T. J. put words to thoughts he had been rolling around in his head for the last day or so.

"Got something on my mind I want to talk to you about," he said, looking over his coffee cup at the boy. "From what I can see you're a good boy and a hard worker. I've got a little place down on the south plains of Texas. It ain't much but it takes a lot of work to keep it going. I could use a good hand. Couldn't pay much, I figure ten dollars a month and keep. Don't know if you'd be interested but thought I'd ask."

Lupe had stopped eating. He sat staring wide-eyed with his mouth open as if he couldn't believe what he was hearing. His mouth worked but no sound came out. He swallowed and swiped watery eyes with the back of a sleeve. Clearing his throat, he tried again to speak.

"Mr. Littlejohn, sir, if you're offering, I'm taking."

They reached across the table and shook hands to seal the bargain.

"Then it's settled," T. J. told him. "We'll leave before first light in the morning."

The Marshal's small office was crowded. More than a dozen of Alamogordo's citizens were there along with T. J. and Lupe. Tom Short stood and held up a hand for silence.

"I sent that telegram to the Sheriff over in Tucson like you said, T. J. I got the answer back awhile ago. It said the reward money would be wired to the Wells Fargo office in Lubbock, Texas like you asked.

"They said all you needed in order to claim the reward was an affidavit, signed by me and three witnesses, saying that we could identify the two men you brought in as the Sanchez brothers. We couldn't agree on just three witnesses, so we figured it wouldn't hurt nothing if there was more than three names on it."

The Marshal handed T. J. a folded piece of paper. "Here's that affidavit and it's signed by every person in the room."

T. J. felt a big lump crawling up the back of his throat. He swallowed hard in a vain attempt to get shed of it, but it just kept hanging there, threatening to choke him. With a shaky hand he reached out and took the offered paper.

"One more thing," the Marshal said. "We hear that Lupe will be going with you and we figured he'd need something to ride. So, the town council got together and decided that pinto and saddle Jose use to ride might serve the purpose. We figure it was most likely stole anyway. And we want you to have the other Sanchez horse and saddle for all you done for our town. They're both waiting outside."

T. J. was speechless. He glanced quickly at his young friend. Lupe seemed beside himself. A huge smile stretched his face.

Darkness still held the land outside in its grasp. Inside the livery stable a lantern cast dim shadows across the hard-packed dirt floor. T. J. adjusted the trail supplies in Samson's packsaddle and tightened the tie down straps. The big brown pack mule had proved true to old Isaac's word, he was trail tough and an easy keeper. T. J. again checked their eight canteens and two water bags to make sure they were secure.They had a lot of desert to cross.

He took time to show Lupe how to lift his new pinto's front leg when he tightened the cinch, then lift it again to give the belly strap a final tightening. "That way your saddle won't be sliding off to one side with you."

"Thanks Mr. Littlejohn," the boy said, clearly excited about heading out on their trip.

They had already said their good-byes to the old liveryman and the town folk but T. J. stuck out a gloved hand again.

"Take care of yourself, old timer."

"You do the same," the old man said, his voice choking. "Take care of the boy too. I got kind of use to having him around."

"You can count on it," T. J. said, giving the lead rope to the rusty-red sorrel with the white blaze face and stockings a wrap around his saddle knob. "Let's ride, boy. We got a far piece to go."

Kneeing the buckskin, they were quickly swallowed up by the darkness. The muffled crunch of their horses' hooves in the soft sand and the rhythmic creak of saddle leather were the only sounds to disturb the early morning quietness as they made their way down the street.

At a lone house at the edge of town, shuttered windows leaked the yellow kerosene light of morning lanterns. A dog barked. A rooster crowed. And T. J. turned the buckskin's nose northeast toward home.

The first rays of sun found them approaching a range of low mountains, beyond that lay a wide stretch of desert country. All day they rode, from dark to dark, riding steadily across the sun-baked desert, picking their way around groves of gnarled mesquite and prickly pear, stopping only occasionally to rest the horses.

T. J. learned two things about Lupe that day. First off he learned the boy was a pretty good saddle pard. Never complained, never lagged behind, always rode stirrup-to-stirrup.

The other thing T. J. learned was that Lupe Ramirez never stopped asking questions. Before T. J. could answer one question the boy already had another halfway out of his mouth.

"Boy, you've talked a steady stream ever since we climbed in the saddle this morning. My jaw is plumb worn out from working so much today, besides, I've about used up all the words I know." That slowed the boy's questions down for maybe a mile or so.

It was well after good dark before they reined into a deep arroyo, found a cutback, and made camp for the night.

"It'll be late tomorrow before we'll be out of this desert," he told the boy. "So go easy on the water. We're in Apache country so there won't be a fire tonight. Reckon we can make do with one of those cold biscuits Miss Sadie sacked up for us and a piece of deer jerky?"

"Sure sounds good to me. How far you reckon we come today, Mr. Littlejohn?"

"Oh, fifty, maybe sixty miles I reckon."

"How far is it to your valley?"

"Another five or six days hard riding, more or less," T. J. told him.

"I've never been this far from town before," Lupe said, lying on his bedroll and propping up on an elbow. "This sure is a big country."

"Yeah, I reckon it is at that. We best get some shut-eye, boy, I want to be up and making tracks before first light."

CHAPTER VII

The children were all asleep. Mary had tossed and turned for over an hour and still hadn't so much as closed her eyes. Letting out a heavy sigh, she swung her feet silently to the floor, wrapped a quilt from the bed around her, and slipped quietly out the front door.

It was a lovely fall evening. A million twinkling stars and a thumbnail moon filled the night sky. A chill was in the air. It wouldn't be long until the first frost. T. J. had promised to be home by then.

But what if he couldn't? What if...NO! I can't let myself think that! Oh, T. J. I miss you so.

Her heart swelled and thundered inside her chest. A sob worked its way up her throat on a sigh. Grief, and worry, and a feeling of helplessness gave birth to tears, tears that overflowed her eyes and scorched hot trails down her cheeks, tears that gushed from what must be a great, bottomless reservoir. She leaned her head against the back of T. J.'s rocker and didn't even bother wiping her tear stained face.

* * *

A rooster crowed.

Mary jerked awake. She blinked herself to awareness and realized she had spent the night on the front porch in T. J.'s rocker.

A growing grayness colored the eastern sky, announcing the dawning of another day. Another day in which she would go about her daily chores, looking up repeatedly at those far hills across the creek, searching, hoping, praying she would see her husband coming.

This is the longest we have ever been apart, Mary thought. *In all the eighteen years we've been married, he's never been away from home this long. If it hurts this bad to be apart just for a few days, how can I possible stand it when he's...*

"Ma," Tad said with concern sounding in his voice and scattering her thoughts. "What're you doing out here still in your nightgown? You been out here all night?"

" I couldn't sleep. Is Marilyn up?"

"Not yet. Want me to go ahead and build a fire?"

"I'll do it. You go ahead and start your chores. I'll put the coffee on and start breakfast. Let's let Marilyn sleep in an extra hour or so this morning. She's been having a hard time for the past few days."

"She sick?"

"No, just woman stuff. Nothing for you to be concerned about."

"Ma, after I get all my chores done, reckon I could go hunting?"

"I suppose that would be all right, but not until all your chores are finished, mind you. Make sure the fresh water barrel on the porch is full too."

"Yes ma'am," he near shouted, excited that he would get to go hunting with his new rifle for the very first time.

Rushing into the house, he grabbed the milk bucket and almost ran over Mary as he hurried to the barn to do the milking and feed the stock. By the time Tad got back to the house with the bucket brimming with fresh milk, breakfast was on the table.

"What you gonna shoot, bubby?" Sally asked around a mouthful of biscuit with honey on it.

"No telling," Tad answered, "When a man goes hunting he never knows what he's going to bring home."

"You ain't no man," she corrected her brother. "You're just my brother."

"Ain't neither! I'm almost fourteen!"

"He ain't no man, is he ma?" She appealed.

"Your father says Tad is more man than most men," she said, casting a sideways look at her son.

"When's Papa coming home, Mother?" Marilyn asked.

"He said it would take a week going and coming. Don't know how long he'll have to be there. I expect it'll be a few more days."

"I sure do miss him," Marilyn said.

"So do I, honey, so do I."

Tad had never felt prouder and more like a grown up man than he did when he left the house with his new Henry rifle tucked comfortably in the crook of his arm. *Think I'll head over toward Short Mountain,* he thought. *Might find me a buck deer in that little box valley.* Looking down, he suddenly realized he was taking longer steps. *Betcha my steps are might near as long as Pa's now.*

Short Mountain was about four miles from the house. He had been there with his pa several times. A small box valley lay on one side of the steep mountain. The entrance was narrow and the other three sides were too steep even for a horse to climb. A natural spring at the box end created a small pond year around. Most every time he and his pa had been there they had spotted several deer grazing on the lush, green grass.

He was still the best part of a quarter mile from the entrance to the little valley when he saw it; someone had fenced off the entrance. A double rail fence stretched from bank to bank. *But why would anybody fence off a little valley way out here?*

The answer became clear a few steps later when he saw at least two dozen cattle grazing contentedly on the fetlock-high grass. *Cattle? What would cattle be doing way out here? Why would someone fence up cattle in this remote place unless...* He stopped dead in his tracks. *These are stolen cattle! These have got to be Jed Holly's cattle, the ones Marshal Paxton was talking about.*

Tad's thoughts swirled. His muscles tightened. *If them are stolen cattle, the cattle thief might be hid somewhere close guarding them.* The thought sent shivers of fear racing up his spine. He hunkered down behind a clump of mulberry bushes. His eyes darted from side-to-side, seeking an unknown enemy. *What would pa do if he was here?*

Tad's thoughts were scattered by the crack of a rifle shot. A slug whistled past his face, so close he could feel the rush of hot air before the bullet ricocheted off a large rock nearby and whined off. His heart leaped into his throat! *Somebody's shooting at me!*

The morning sun had arched halfway to noon-high when T. J. spotted them. There were three of them—Apache. They walked their mounts over the top of a ridge maybe a quarter mile to his left and sky lined themselves, obviously wanting to be seen. They reined to a stop and for a long few minutes sat their ponies, sizing up their query like a cougar would a newborn calf. After awhile, they turned and rode slowly along the ridge, biding their time. They would slit a man's throat for the boots he wore or the horse he rode and they were in no hurry.

"Mr. Littlejohn," the boy whispered loudly, "there's some Indians over yonder!"

"I see 'em, boy."

"What are we gonna do?" Lupe asked breathlessly.

"We ain't gonna do nothing."

"But shouldn't we make a run for it or something?"

"Son, with Apaches, it ain't the ones you see that you worry about, it's the ones you don't see. You don't see an Apache unless he wants you to see him."

"What do they want, then?"

"Most likely our horses. They just haven't figured out yet how to get them without a fight."

"Ain't no Indian gonna take my pinto," Lupe said emphatically.

"Then we best sleep with one eye open tonight."

All day the three Apaches dogged their trail, sometimes following in clear view, sometimes not showing themselves for an hour or more, but always there. Twice that day T. J. had to stop and hurry off into the bushes with a coughing spell, vomiting up blood each time. Each time it drained precious energy from his body. He didn't want the boy to see it.

The sun was dipping near the western horizon before the Indians seemed to vanish, but T. J. knew from experience they hadn't given up. If there was one thing every Apache had, it was patience.

For the best part of an hour T. J. had been following a river as it snaked its way sluggishly across the desert countryside. Both banks were brushy, choked with groves of scraggly willow and wind-tossed scrub cedar. Cactus and Agave clung to thin topsoil. Slender mesquite trees bent sharply, twisted by the swirling canyon winds.

In places, the persistent water had carved out gorges through a line of low mountains, leaving high banks that reached fifty feet or more toward the sky. The land was harsh, untamed, and seldom saw human activity.

It was nearing last light when he found the place he had been looking for. The river had cut a deep opening through a steep mountain, leaving a sheer cliff, maybe forty feet high, on the left side. The river had receded from the right side leaving a sloping, sandy bank strewn with huge, water-washed boulders. Behind the boulders rose another cliff face that climbed sharply.

"This will do just fine," T. J. said, reining the buckskin down into the opening. "We'll camp here tonight."

Picking their way through the large rocks he found a small clearing and reined into it.

"How about unsaddling and watering our stock while I rustle up some driftwood for a fire," he asked the boy. "Don't know about you but my belt buckle is rubbing my backbone. I could use some grub."

"But ain't you afraid those Indians will see a fire and find us again?"

"They ain't never lost us. They know where we are. No use us doing without supper. Never did like fighting Apache on an empty stomach."

"You think they will come tonight?" Lupe asked, fear sounding in his words.

"They'll come. Shore as God made green apples, they'll come."

By the time Lupe finished watering the horses from the river, T. J. had a fire going and coffee boiling. He shaved salt pork into a frying pan and sliced four potatoes in on top.

"We'll picket the horses back there between us and that cliff. That way they'll have to come past us to get to them," T. J. said. "Ain't likely, but just maybe they'll look the layout over and decide it ain't worth the effort. Spread our bedrolls here close to the fire.

"When you figure they'll come, Mr. Littlejohn?"

"Hard to say, best guess is sometime toward morning."

T. J. used his long hunting knife to scrape half of the potatoes and salt pork from the frying pan into a tin plate and handed it to the boy. He poured both of them a cup of steaming coffee and folded cross-legged to the sand beside the campfire.

Lupe sat across the fire, picking at his food and glancing about, peering nervously into the deepening darkness. His head snapped up at every sound. His dark eyes flicked to and fro, searching for their unseen enemy.

"Better eat your supper, boy. Worrying never changes nothing."

After supper they scrubbed their cooking pans with sand and washed them in the river before repacking them. T. J. slid the Henry rifle from its saddle boot and fed its hungry belly full of cartridges. He broke open the double-barrel shotgun, thumbed two shells in, and then snapped it closed with a flick of his wrist. Laying the weapons within easy reach, he settled down beside the fire with another cup of coffee.

It was a beautiful night. Dark settled in. Firelight filled the small clearing with an amber glow. The moon wasn't full, but nearly so; it, and a sky full of stars, bathed the gorge with darkening degrees of eerie gray. The gurgling water of the river made a peaceful sound and belied the danger that lurked somewhere out there in the night. Off in the distance the lonesome cry of a coyote carried to them on a warm, dry breeze through the night. Another answered.

"You ever been scared, Mr. Littlejohn?

"Lots of times. A man that says otherwise is a liar."

"Are you sick?"

"Seems so."

"Are...are you gonna die?"

"We're all gonna die, boy, some sooner than others. Reckon the good Lord just seen fit to tell me when my time was coming.

"Do you, do you worry about dying?"

"Some. Right now we better get some rest, it's likely to be a long night."

Sheriff Paxton was worried. He shifted uncomfortably in the saddle. His eyes swept the ground as he rode. He had just left Homer Green's place. First, a dozen of Jed Holly's cattle turned up missing and now some of Homer's cows were gone too. On top of that, Homer said he had seen three hardcase strangers nosing around.

The only other spread within twenty miles was T. J.'s place. Pulling his hat down tighter, he touched heels to his gray's flanks and urged the mare into a ground eating, short lope.

The sun was a notch past noon-high when he topped the rise and headed down the sloping hill into T. J.'s valley. From appearances, everything seemed normal: A small herd of cattle grazed peacefully on the valley's lush grass. A team of mules milled about in the corral. Little Sally was swinging under the big Oak tree and Mary seemed to be working in a small flower garden near the front porch.

Reining his horse to a stop at water's edge he allowed the mare to slake its thirst from the fresh, clear water of the running creek. Pulling the makings from a shirt pocket, he sat his saddle and rolled himself a smoke.

George felt bad about T. J., they had been friends over twenty years. When Alice was alive they had exchanged visits several times with T. J. and Mary. Most folks around Lubbock pretty much shunned the Littlejohn's, using the excuse that he was a half-breed, but George suspected it was more about his looks; he wasn't easy to look at until you got to know him.

It suddenly dawned on him that the thought of Alice hadn't brought the stab of pain to his heart that he had grown use to over the past, almost three years. He still loved her, always would, but the hurt was healing.

He pulled a deep inhale of smoke into his lungs and felt the pleasurable biting sensation that had become a habit. Alice never had liked for him to smoke and had nagged him about it constantly. He still felt a tinge of guilt every time he lit up. *She shore was a good woman though.*

His green eyes flicked up at the thought and locked on Mary Littlejohn. She knelt on her hands and knees, pulling grass from the flowerbed. She wore a gray and white checkered, ankle-length work dress with a white apron tied around her waist. Her long, golden hair hung in a plait down her back to near her waist. *There's another good woman and she's shore pleasing to look at to boot.*

Sighing heavily, he flicked the half-smoked cigarette into the water and kneed his mare forward and splashed across the creek.

Sally must have spotted him because he saw Mary suddenly shoot a look over her shoulder and spring to her feet. She shielded her eyes with the palm of her hand, then, obviously recognizing him, lifted it just above shoulder-high in a friendly greeting.

Drawing near, he touched thumb and finger to his hat brim. "Afternoon, Mrs. Littlejohn."

"Good Afternoon, George. What are doing out this way again so soon?"

"Had to ride over to Homer Green's place. Seems some of his cows are missing too. You folks haven't lost any cattle lately have you?"

"Not that I know of. That's part of Tad's chores to count the stock every day. I'm sure he would have said something if any of them had been missing. Is something wrong?"

"Can't be sure yet, but Homer said he spotted three saddle tramps hanging around his neck of the woods. You folks haven't seen any strangers hereabouts have you?"

"No, we haven't seen a soul. Is it something we should be concerned about?"

"Most likely not, but with T. J. gone, I'd keep the kids close for awhile."

Mary caught her breath in a sharp gasp of air. Her hand flew to cover her mouth. "Oh, heavens!"

"What's wrong ma'am?"

"I let Tad go hunting with his new rifle this morning."

Worry wrinkled the sheriff's forehead. "I wouldn't be too concerned, ma'am. Tad's a fine boy. How long has he been gone?"

"He left early this morning, right after breakfast," she told him, feeling a tight knot of fear coiling in the pit of her stomach. "He should be back by now."

"Do you know which way he went?"

"He said something about Short Mountain, about four miles northeast."

"Yeah, I know the place," he said, trying not to let the concern he was feeling come through in his voice. "He's probably got himself a big buck deer and having to field dress it. Tell you what, I'll just mosey over that way and see if I can give him a hand."

George touched his hat brim with a curled finger and reined around. Heeling the mare's flanks, he urged his mount into a trot.

When he got out of sight of the house he yanked his hat down tight around his ears, relaxed the reins and put his mount into a hard gallop. Weaving through and around groves of sycamore, he kept the mare headed northeast. It took less than a half an hour to cover the four miles. He spotted the mountain up ahead just as he heard two rifle shots. He knew instantly Tad was in trouble Those weren't the shots of a hunter shooting at a deer. Leaning back in the saddle, he snaked his Henry rifle from the backward saddle boot and levered a shell as he rode.

With the gray running full out, belly to the ground, he broke out of the trees. His gaze swept a quick circle in front of him. A puff of smoke from a rifle on the left hillside caught his attention. An answering shot from behind a big rock to the right told him the location of another person. *Is that one Tad?* He took a chance and swung his mount that direction.

Leaning low in the saddle and riding hard he crooked his neck and watched the hillside. The shooter on the hillside fired again, another puff of smoke reeled away on the wind and a bullet bit a chip out of the saddle horn only inches from his stomach.

Twisting in the saddle he brought his Henry to shoulder and snapped off a hasty shot in the general direction of the shooter. He hauled back on the reins and jerked his mount to a sliding stop even as he swung a leg over the saddle. He hit the ground running.

He spotted Tad hunkered down behind the huge boulder. George covered the twenty feet or so in a few long bounds and dove headlong the last few yards. It was none too soon. A slug ricocheted off the rock and whined past his cheek as he belly-flopped beside Tad.

The boy's face was drenched with beads of sweat as he sat with his back against the rock.

"You okay, boy?" the sheriff asked as soon as he could get his breath.

"Yes sir" The surprisingly calm voice replied.

"Got any idea who that is up there shooting at us?"

"No sir, but I figure it's a cattle rustler guarding them cattle over yonder."

"Yeah, I think you're right," the sheriff said, tugging off his hat and dragging a sleeve across his sweat-drenched forehead.

Glancing down at the brand new rifle in Tad's hands he pointed a nod at it and fixed the young hunter with a stare.

"You as good with that thing as T. J. says?"

"Pa taught me to shoot. He says I got a knack for it."

"Son, if we're gonna get out of this with our hides intact

you're gonna have to help me. I ain't breathed this to a living soul, but my eyes ain't what they use to be. I doubt I could hit that boulder that fellow is hiding behind, much less him. I reckon it falls on you to do it. Think you can shoot a man that's trying to shoot us?"

For a long minute Tad stared silently at a spot between his feet. The sheriff could tell the boy was struggling inside himself. Then, with his head still lowered, he nodded his head just once, just like George had seen T. J. do a thousand times.

"I can do it."

"Okay, then here's what we're gonna do," the sheriff explained. "I'm gonna put my hat on the end of my rifle and slowly raise it up on the left side of this rock so that fellow up there can see it. You belly down on the right side and be ready. He'll have to raise up to get a crack at me. You won't have but one shot, make it good, understand?"

"Yes sir."

"Remember, Tad, that shooter up there will kill us both if we don't kill him first. Don't freeze up on that trigger. You ready?"

"Yes sir."

"Then here we go," the sheriff said, balancing his dark brown Stetson on the nose of his rifle.

Tad bellied down flat to the ground and levered a shell into his Henry. His mind whirled. A lump that felt like the size of his fist was stuck in his throat. He swallowed hard. His gut tightened. His hand made sweat on the stock of his rifle and he took time to wipe it on his pant leg.

Sick, hot dread surged through him like a flood as the realization burst somewhere in his head. *I'm fixing to kill a man. Can I do it? Can I squeeze the trigger when the time comes?* Then he remembered what his pa had told him. *'Son, you're more of a man than most men. A man's gotta do what a man's gotta do.*

He sucked up a bellyful of air and let it out in a slow slide just like his pa taught him. His finger touched the trigger like a butterfly lighting on a flower. He blinked his eyes clear.

"I'm ready, Mr. Paxton."

CHAPTER VIII

T ime crept slowly. Minutes felt like hours, hours like days, and still Mary and Marilyn and Sally sat on the porch where they had been since the sheriff rode away. They stared silently off at the distant hills, watching, waiting, praying. Their eyes burned. Their hearts ached. As time slipped away, so did their hopes, like sand sifting through their fingers.

Then, like a mirage through the afternoon heat's haze, they appeared—two horses on the distant hill across the creek. Mary came to her feet. She shielded her eyes and squinted. There was no mistaking the gray horse, it was Sheriff Paxton. But the other horse carried something, or someone, draped across the saddle.

Mary stood motionless, barely breathing, her hand clutched her mouth as if to hold back the scream that threatened to escape her throat. Her hands went cold. Her stomach churned. "Please, God, please, don't let it be Tad," she murmured over and over.

As the horses drew near the creek they reined up. Sheriff Paxton leaned over and tied the reins of the extra horse to a low-hanging limb. Only then did Mary realize someone was riding double with the sheriff, and it was Tad!

Like a shot she was off the porch, running, her skirts flying. Marilyn and Sally were right behind her. Relief, excitement, and a tide of overwhelming gratitude grew with every footfall.

Through happy tears she saw her son slide from the back of the gray horse, rifle in hand, and race to meet her. The distance between them closed. They clashed into each other's arms. Mary drew her son to her breasts, crushing him in a mother's embrace, and closed her eyes in a silent prayer of thankfulness.

It caused quite a commotion when the sheriff rode into Lubbock. Townspeople stopped what they were doing and stared as George Paxton rode slowly down the dusty street on his gray mare. Behind him, he led a bay gelding. A dead man was tied belly down across the saddle.

Little plumes of dust puffed away from the horses' hooves and hung there in the growing grayness of dusk. A dog scampered from under the boardwalk and trailed the two horses, barking at their heels. The insistent ringing of Old Isaac's blacksmith hammer fell silent. Mothers pulled their children close.

"Who you got there, Sheriff?" Wiley Stubblefield, the storekeeper hollered. He received no reply.

"Wonder who that fellow is?" Someone asked, the question directed at no one.

Reining up in front of the undertakers office, George swung a tired leg over his saddle and stepped to the ground.

"Who is he, Sheriff?" somebody from the growing wad of people shouted. He paid them no mind and handed the reins to the bay to Marvin Tucker, the Undertaker.

"Got a fellow that needs burying, Marvin."

"I'd say that's a fair statement," the undertaker said as he lifted the dead man's head and stared at his face.

"Couple of you fellows give him a hand here," Sheriff Paxton said, looping the reins to his gray over a hitching rail.

"Holy Smoke!" one of the men helping get the corpse off the horse said excitedly. "Would you look at that? One bullet right between the eyes. That's some kind of shooting, Sheriff!"

"I'll give you what I know after awhile, Marvin," George said. "Don't know the jasper's name. Meantime, just put it down as, *cattle rustler.*

"I'll take your horse down to the livery as I go, Sheriff," old Silas, the liveryman told him. "You look plumb tuckered out."

"It's been a long day. Got to ride out to see Jed Holly and Homer Green first thing in the morning. It was their cattle this fellow was rustling."

He brushed off a dozen questions as he strode wearily through the growing darkness to his office. He lit the coal oil lamp and slumped into his chair just as the 'Honorable' Albert R. Pennington, the Governor's new appointment for Lubbock County Judge hurried through the door. As usual, he had a cockleburr under his saddle.

"I hear you just brought in a dead man, Sheriff?"

"Reckon you heard right, Judge."

"Who was he?"

"Don't know yet. He was a cattle rustler, that's all I know about him right now."

"I heard you shot him between the eyes, is that true?"

"I'll turn in my report in the morning. Right now I'm gonna kick my boots off and get some rest, I'm worn out."

"Did you have to kill him? Why didn't you just arrest him and bring him in for trial? I'm beginning to think you have the idea you are judge, jury, *and* executioner."

"Judge, you're new in town so I'm gonna cut you some slack this time. I don't tell you how to do your job, don't try to tell me how to do mine. Now get outta here before I forget my manners."

"I'm warning you, *Sheriff,* there'll be an inquest," the man gritted, his face so red you could might-near light a cigarette on it. "For your sake, I hope you can *prove* your shooting of that man was justified. I'll expect your report on my desk first thing in the morning."

If I had a lick of sense I'd get out of law work, he thought as the judge stormed out of the office. *He's about the sorriest excuse for a judge I ever seen, probably the Governor's kinfolk or something.*

Down the street in front of the saloon, two men slouched against a post and sipped the mug of beer in their hands. They had watched all the events ever since the Sheriff rode in.

"What we gonna do, Bob?" one of them whispered in a bullfrog voice to his companion. "That was our own brother strung across that saddle."

The speaker was a bearded giant, thick chested and broad shouldered, built like a mountain grizzly. A battered, floppy hat with a feather in the band was pulled down tight over scraggly hair that hung well below his collar. His matted and dirty, dark brown hair and beard met in the middle to hide his face. A tobacco streak marked the edge of his mouth on both sides. Only his alcohol-blurred eyes were visible.

The other man was tall and thin. His emerald-green eyes seemed to bug out of a leathery face, cooked that way by a lifetime in the sun. A slash of mouth curled down at one side in a perpetual snarl. His right hand rested on a tied down Walker Colt in a low-cut holster tied low on his hip, the sure mark of one who fancies himself a gunfighter.

"Do?" he questioned without diverting his steady gaze at the Sheriff's office down the street. "What do you think we're gonna do, Amos? We're gonna *kill* the one that killed young Billy, that's what we're gonna *do*."

"I knowed that! But what're we waiting on? That fellow's right down there by hisself, let's jest go down and shoot him dead." The big man said, flicking a look about to make sure they weren't being overheard. "I mean, what we gonna do about burying Billy?"

"What you want me to do, dig the grave? I feel as bad about Billy as you do, but getting ourselves throwed in jail or killed ain't gonna help get the one that done it. Besides, dead is dead. Ain't nothing gonna change that."

"I know, but it just don't seem right. Ma would want us to put a name on his grave."

"Ma's dead, Amos, and if you keep shooting your mouth off, we might end up buried in a hole right next to Billy. That sheriff ain't no greenhorn. You heard how Billy had a bullet hole square between his eyes. Shut up and come on, I need another drink."

The sheriff was still tired when he swung his feet to a cold floor and pushed up from his little cot in back of his office. He lit the lamp, yawned, stretched, and wiped sleep from his eyes as he staggered barefooted to the potbellied stove in the corner. Opening the squeaky door, he stirred red coals with a poker and coaxed a fire to life, then threw in a couple pieces of wood from a stack behind the stove.

He shook the blackened pot to make sure there was left over coffee and set it on the stove to heat.

After dressing and stomping on his boots and a trip out back to the outhouse, he poured water into a wash pan and washed his face, lathered up, whetted his straight razor on a razor strap, and scraped off yesterday's stubble. Hearing the coffee boiling, he wiped his face with a towel and poured himself a cup. The steaming liquid was so hot it nearly scaled the hide off his tongue.

Reaching a hand, he took down his gunbelt and holster from the peg on the wall, swung it around his waist, and buckled it in place. Then, as he had done every morning for most of his life, he routinely withdrew his pistol, checked the load, and returned it to its place.

He dreaded the long ride back out to Jed and Homers, it meant another whole day in the saddle, but they would be wanting to go pick up their stolen cattle. Picking up the report from his desk, he settled down in his chair to go over it one more time.

It had been well past midnight when he finally finished his account leading to the death of the cattle rustler. He hated to put down the truth about the events out at Short Mountain. He had been tempted to lie, to say it was his shot that killed the rustler, not Tad's. He hated to saddle the boy with the stigma of killing a man, even if it was to save both their lives, but in the end, he knew he had no choice, he had to tell the truth. Sighing heavily, he lifted from his chair, scooped up the report and his hat and headed out the door.

It was good light but the sun was sleeping in. George aimed a look up at a clear sky then let his gaze do a quick sweep of the street. Lubbock was waking up: Wiley was sweeping the boardwalk in front of his store; old Silas was already banging on his anvil; a freight wagon lumbered past.

"Morning, Sheriff. Where you off to this morning?"

"Morning, Wiley. Got to ride out to Jed and Homer's place. It was their cattle that fellow was stealing. Want to do me a favor and see the judge gets this report when he comes by?"

"Be glad to. You shore done a good job with that fellow, Sheriff. He won't be rustling any more cattle."

Without replying, George turned and headed for the livery.

Silas looked up from shaping a horseshoe and laid his hammer down as the sheriff strode up.

"I went ahead and saddled your gray."

"Much obliged."

"Know who that fellow was yet?"

"Nope."

"Couple of, no-goods in town, rode in yesterday morning. Thought you'd want to know. That's their horses there in the corral. Both slat-ribbed and starved half to death. Way a fellow takes care of his horse tells me a lot about the man."

"Where they staying?"

"Reckon they're at the hotel, seen them headed that way."

"I'll check them out when I get back, most likely be dark or better though," he said as he stuck a boot in a stirrup and swung into the saddle.

"You ride easy, George."

Two strangers in town, he thought as he rode up the street. *Homer said he saw three fellows nosing around near his place before he lost his cows. Reckon they could be the dead man's partners? I'll talk to them when I get back tonight.*

The morning was half spent when the Dutton brothers left the Lubbock café and headed for the saloon. Pushing through the bat-wings they selected a table near the back and scraped out chairs. They were the only customers in the place.

"Give us a couple of beers over here," Amos Dutton snarled in his husky voice.

"I don't wait tables," the bartender told him gruffly. "You want a beer, come and get 'em."

The big giant's massive head shot around angrily. Bob knew his brother's razor-edge temper had a hair trigger and lifted a hand to halt him halfway out of his chair.

"Shut up and sit down, Amos. I'll handle it," he whispered. "We don't want no trouble."

Nursing their beers, the two brothers watched a dozen or more townspeople come and go over the next hour. Bob had just walked over to the bar to get them another round when a balding fellow wearing sleeve suspenders hurried in and bellied up to the bar.

"What'll you have, Frank, the usual?" The bartender asked, casually sitting a glass on the bar and snatching a bottle to pour.

"Make it a double," the man said breathlessly. "I was cutting that new judge's hair just now and you'll never guess what he told me."

"Hope he told you he was resigning. He's a hard fellow to like."

"Nope," the man said smugly. "He told me the sheriff wasn't the one that shot that fellow."

The bartender's furrowed face and lowered eyebrows conveyed his disbelief as he continued pouring whiskey into the glass in front of the town barber.

"Well, did he say who did then?"

"It was that half-breed's boy, Tad Littlejohn. He's the one that put that bullet between that fellow's eyes. Done it from over a hundred yards away."

"Yeah, and a pig can fly too."

"It's the gospel truth. I didn't believe it myself at first, but the judge showed me the sheriff's report. It tells all about what happened."

"How old is that boy? Haven't seen him in town in a couple of years."

"I run into Doc on the way over here and was telling him about it. He says the boy is coming up on fourteen."

"Hard to believe a boy that young could shoot like that," the bartender said. "Even if he is part Indian. Where did this ruckus take place anyway?"

"According to the sheriff's report, it all happened over by Short Mountain, that's about twenty miles northwest of here and only a few miles from the Littlejohn place."

"Yeah, well, I still have a hard time believing a fourteen-year-old kid can shoot like that, must have been a lucky shot."

"Maybe, but that fellow is just as dead."

"Yeah, you're shore 'nuff right about that."

Bob Dutton had heard enough. He pushed away from the bar, his mind spinning. "Think we'll pass on another round, barkeep. Reckon we've had enough for today, we've got a long ways to ride."

Outside, the Dutton brothers headed quickly for the hotel, gathered their gear, and walked hurriedly down the street to the livery.

"What you in such an all fired hurry for, Bob. Where we going? I need another beer."

"Shut up and get your horse saddled. We're gonna pay some folks a little visit."

T. J. had catnapped all night, examining every sound, identifying every scent, every sense on its highest alert, careful to keep his eyes closed in the knowledge that even the briefest glance at the moon or stars would temporarily blind him to the darkness.

In the deepest part of the night they came. No sound detectable to human ears betrayed their coming, but Solomon heard. A low snort deep in the mule's chest announced the Apaches' approach. T. J.'s right hand crept stealthily to clamp over Lupe's mouth to stifle the natural sound one makes when awakened suddenly. The boy's dark eyes snapped open wide in fright then seemed to relax as T. J. crossed his lips with a finger.

With his left hand he thumbed back the twin hammers on the Stevens double-barrel shotgun and slipped the rawhide loop over his left wrist. His hand found the Henry rifle lying beside him and drew it close. He was as ready as he would ever be. Silence deepened.

Then he heard it, like the faintest hint of a bird in flight, a feathered swish sped through the dim, graying darkness, then another. T. J.'s gut tightened. The two Apache arrows found their mark and embedded deep into the two bedrolls near the dying embers of last night's campfire.

Good thing we spent the night over here behind this rock instead of in them bunched-up bedrolls, he thought, *we'd be buzzard bait right now.*

A rifle exploded from behind a low line of rocks only thirty yards or so from the campfire. A finger of fire drew a line in the darkness and marked the shooter's location. A second shot followed closely behind the first. Two soft thuds bit into the bedrolls.

From the short space of time between the two shots, that's got to be a lever action repeater. He reasoned. *It's got the sound of a Henry.*

T. J.'s years fighting Apache told him what would likely come next and he braced himself. They erupted from behind the rocks as if the ground suddenly gave birth to three grown men. Their forms were silhouetted against the gray sky background. Their bodies were naked except for a breechcloth and knee-high moccasins. Their greased skin glistened in the moon's glow.

One clutched a rifle in both hands as they approached cautiously. Another carried a tomahawk and the third held a long lance with a knife lashed to the business end. As they drew near the two empty bedrolls, the one with the lance probed the rolled-up blanket with the tip of his lance. With a muttered voice he sounded the alarm. All three dropped into a crouch.

Raising up from behind his rock, T. J. brought his Henry to shoulder and found the one with the rifle before levering a shell. All three would-be assassins stiffened and spun around. T. J. feathered the trigger. The bullet from his Henry smacked into the Apache's chest with a muffled sound like a hand striking a baby's bottom. The man dropped his rifle and staggered backwards before falling flat of his back.

Jacking another shell, T. J. fired just as the second target twisted his body. The .44 slug ripped into the man, wounding him in the side. Emitting a low grunt, the warrior wheeled and sprinted for the safety of the nearby rocks.

For a long moment the remaining Apache seemed to hesitate in indecision as if his warrior upbringing was battling with his will to live and his mind was the battlefield. Years of training won out. He let out a bloodcurdling death scream and charged directly at T. J. With ferocity the warrior scribed a long arc over his right shoulder with the tomahawk. Moonlight reflected off the shiny metal as it began its decent.

The move caught T. J. by surprise. He didn't have time to chamber another shell or make use of the sawed-off shotgun dangling from his left wrist. By sheer instinct he swung his rifle up to ward off the blow. The force of the impact jarred up T. J.'s arm and bashed the rifle from his grasp. The Apache set his feet and snarled wickedly, and raised his tomahawk for the final blow. T. J. stiffened to accept his fate.

From the darkness beside him a pistol barked. The Indian stiffened. The tomahawk dropped to the ground as his hand clutched at the hole in his stomach. Dark liquid leaked between his fingers as he turned and staggered away into the darkness like a wounded animal.

Turning, T. J. stared into Lupe's wide-eyed, terror filled face. The boy clutched a smoking pistol in his white-knuckled fist. Off in the distant darkness the galloping hooves of two unshod ponies faded into the desert night.

CHAPTER IX

The sun dipped westward. The afternoon was half spent. Two men lay on their bellies in a thick stand of low-lying cedar, which hugged the shoulder of a hill overlooking Yellow House Creek. For half an hour they lay quietly, staring intently at the cabin in the valley below.

"You fer shore this is where the half-breed lives?" Amos Dutton asked, clearly irritated at what he considered a waste of time.

"I'm sure," his brother replied.

"Then what in tarnation we waitin' on? Let's jest ride on down and do what we come to do."

"If you're in such an all fired hurry you just ride on down, Amos. You might just get a bullet between your eyes like Billy did. So far, I've seen the woman and three kids, but I still ain't seen that half-breed husband."

"We jest gonna kill the kid that shot Billy or we gonna do 'em all?"

"You want to leave witnesses around to put a rope around your neck? No, we ain't leaving nobody to point a finger at us, we'll get rid of the whole family while we're at it."

"Can I do some of them with my knife? Can I Bob?"

* * *

An uneasy feeling gnawed at Mary Littlejohn's stomach. She looked up, wondering, unusually nervous for some unknown reason. Since T. J. left the days had crawled by with agonizing slowness and she had become more and more on edge. She had never been particularly frightened living in their remote valley, even when T. J. was gone, but something was different about today. Some ominous intuition, some sinister evil hung in the air like a dark cloud.

She laid aside the spoon she had been stirring the pot of turnip greens with. To relieve her mind of the uneasy feeling, she walked to the door and passed a roaming gaze around. Sally was in her tree swing as usual. Marilyn was picking butter beans from the garden to put up for the winter, and Tad was splitting wood at the end of the house. *I'm just imagining things,* she tried to tell herself.

Then something caught her eye off in the distance near the creek. Two riders splashed across the ford and up the bank on the near side. They were headed directly toward the house. Cupping a hand to shield her eyes from the sun, she peered at them for a small moment. They were strangers. Mary tensed.

"Tad!" She called urgently. "Riders coming! Get Marilyn and Sally in the house. Quickly!"

As his father had taught him, Tad was never far from his rifle and now he scooped it from its leaning position against the end of the house, alerted Marilyn, and quickly gathered Sally from the swing. Marilyn took Sally's hand and hurried her into the house. Mary held her gaze on the approaching strangers. One was a huge man with scraggly hair and beard that hid his face under a floppy hat. The other was his opposite, tall and skinny. She didn't like the looks of either one.

"Help Marilyn shutter the windows," she told her son. "I've got a bad feeling about those two."

"Afternoon, Ma'am," the skinny one called out as they walked their horses nearer.

Mary edged backwards to stand just inside the door. She felt Tad standing behind her with his rifle in his hands.

"Who are you and what do you want?" she said, trying desperately to keep her voice calmer than she felt.

"I'm Bob Dutton, Ma'am. This here is my brother, Amos. We're just riding through on our way to Lubbock. Seems we took a wrong turn. Wondering if you'd tell us which way it might be?"

"About twenty miles south."

"I do declare, Ma'am, would that be turnip greens I smell cooking? Our ma used to cook turnip greens. I reckon I could eat a bushel. We've been riding all day and we're starved half to death. A plate of them greens sure would set well. Mind if we climb down and stretch our legs," he said, swinging a leg over his saddle.

Behind her, Tad levered a shell into his rifle and stepped into the doorway beside her. The sound of it stopped the man in the middle of dismounting.

"Yes, we do mind," Mary told him firmly. "You should know you don't get off your horse at someone's house unless you're invited. I've told you the way to Lubbock, now be on your way. My husband will be home any minute."

The man hesitated for a long moment before settling back into his saddle. He stared coldly, then an evil grin slit his face.

"Now, boy, that's not at all neighborly. You best put that rifle down before I take offense."

"My ma told you to be on your way."

"We don't take no orders from women or kids," The giant blurted out angrily in his deep voice, suddenly jumping from his saddle and barreling towards Mary and Tad.

Tad deliberately lowered the nose of his rifle and squeezed off a shot. The bullet gouged a furrow in the ground at the big man's feet. Mary jumped backwards through the door. Tad was right behind her and slammed the door just as a bullet from the tall stranger's pistol plowed into the heavy wood of the door. Tad grabbed the wooden bar and dropped it in place only an instant before the giant hit the door with a shoulder. The heavy plank door shuddered on its hinges but held. Sally screamed. Mary grabbed the long-barreled shotgun from the pegs above the door.

"Now, Ma'am. You might as well open that door," a cold, mocking voice called from outside the door. "You folks are making Amos mad, and when he gets mad, he gets real mean. No telling what he might do. Your boy shot our brother yesterday and he's gotta pay."

Mary flicked a frantic look at Tad. In his face she saw a grim determination she had never seen before, something far beyond his years. He levered another shell into his Henry.

Two quick steps took Tad to the shuttered window overlooking the porch. Peeking through the gunport, he saw the burly stranger gathering kindling from the woodpile. Then it hit him—they intended to burn them out.

Ramming the nose of his rifle through the hole, he pointed it in the big man's general direction and fired. A loud roar that sounded like a wounded grizzly bear and a rush of movement outside told Tad his shot had not been in vain. He had gotten lucky.

Withdrawing his rifle, he chanced a quick look. The giant's huge hand was grasping his left leg, just below his hip, trying vainly to stem the spurts of blood squirting between his fingers. A stream of hoarse curses spewed from his mouth.

"That kid done shot me!" the man bellowed.

For a few long minutes all was deathly quiet. However, Tad's satisfying feeling was short lived

"I smell smoke!" Mary whispered frantically, her voice breaking with panic. "Tad! They've set fire to the house!"

* * *

A hint of blue already marked the coming dawn and blotted out the stars. The moon had long since slipped behind the horizon. T. J. and Lupe rode silently. Seemingly, both were replaying the events of less than an hour before.

The soft sand along the riverbank muffled their three horses and pack mule's hooves as they rode away from the place of battle without looking back. Lupe proudly clutched the Henry rifle recovered from the fatally wounded Indian. In T. J.'s eyes, the boy had grown a heap since last night.

Above them, three dark shadows stood out against the lightening sky and scored lazy circles high and slow in a cloudless dawn, dropping lower with each pass. Soon, their brothers would join them for a feast on the fallen warrior.

T. J. felt a growing pain in his lower back and his stomach was rebelling even to the water he had drank from the river as they watered their horses. He still resisted taking the laudanum painkiller the doctor had given him. He figured he would need it a whole lot more later on than he did now.

"We'll stop after awhile and eat a bite," he told the kid riding by his side. "You done good back there."

"I never shot a man before."

"A man's gotta do what a man's gotta do," T. J. told him, his words closing the subject.

The sun had climbed halfway to high when T. J. reined up in the shade of a wide sycamore. A small spring bubbled out from under a rock ledge and trickled a trail through the rocky landscape. Up ahead, a string of mountains stretched like a column of humpbacked monsters marching across the desert. Fingers of outcroppings pointed to the blue Texas sky that seemed to stretch on forever. They were getting closer to home.

"Let's lite and spell the horses," he told the boy. "Don't know about you, but I've been thinking about the last of them cold biscuits. My stomach's been fussing at me for the last couple of hours."

Lupe loosened the cinches and watered their winded horses and let them munch the clumps of green grass along the small stream while T. J. dug the biscuits and jerky from a saddlebag. Both of them stretched out in the cool shade and ate their lunch in silence.

"Mr. Littlejohn," the boy finally said. "I shore appreciate you bringing me along. You won't be sorry. I'll make you a good hand."

"I reckon you earned your keep when you saved my bacon back there. Wasn't for you, them buzzards would be picking my eyeballs out by now."

"I was just thinking, a few days ago I weren't nothing but the town joke. Didn't even have a change of clothes to my name let alone anything else. Now just look, here I am with a real job, a passel of new friends, as fine a horse as ever walked, and a brand new rifle. Life shore takes some twists and turns don't it?"

Lupe's question burned into T. J.'s mind like a red-hot branding iron. For a long few minutes neither spoke. Stillness hung thick in the air like a chill on a frosty morning. *Twists and turns? Yeah, don't it though.* His mind gave birth to familiar thoughts: Thoughts of home, thoughts of Mary and the children, thoughts of their future without him.

"We best be making tracks," he said hoarsely around the lump in his throat.

* * *

George Paxton hooked a leg around his saddle horn and rolled himself a smoke as he watched Jed Holly drop a loop around a post and pull the makeshift fence down. Homer Green and his hired hand, Lester Milam, were coaxing the small herd of cattle from the little valley toward the opening in the fence.

Shore will be glad when all this rustling business is over and done with, he thought as he swiped a match across his pant leg and lit up. He drew in a long inhale and let the blue smoke trickle out in a slow slide.

He was still bothered by the news Silas had shared with him that morning about the two strangers in town. *Soon as I get back I'm gonna check those two out. That fellow Tad shot, no way he could have rustled these cows by himself. He had to have help, most likely his partners left him here to nurse the herd while they rode in to wet their whistle.*

Glancing up at the sun to figure the time, he saw something off to the south that widened his eyes and drove a chill down his spine. *Smoke! That's coming from Littlejohn's valley!*

Discarding the cigarette and swinging his leg down, he lifted high in the saddle and swept off his hat, waving it in the air to get the other's attention.

"Jed!" He shouted and pointed to the line of black smoke trailing skyward off in the distance. "Looks like a fire over at T. J.'s place! We better go see what's going on. Bring Homer and leave Lester here with the cattle. Let's ride!"

Clamping his hat down tightly and jamming spurs to his gray mare, he tore out at a hard gallop. He could hear Jed and Homer hanging close behind him. Riding full out, they covered the four miles to Littlejohn's valley in record time. As they rode they kept a weary eye to the sky; the column of smoke was growing bigger and blacker by the minute.

Topping the hill and tearing down the other side, they could see it was the house. Bright orange flames billowed up from one end, licking at the roof and eating their way through the heavy logs of the sturdy cabin.

As the sheriff and his two companions splashed across the creek and raced toward the house, two men made a dash from the open door of the barn, ducked around the corner, and climbed into their saddles. One seemed to be having trouble with his left leg like he was wounded or something. The other one wheeled his horse and snapped off a shot in their direction. A bullet burned the air.

Pulling iron, George smoked a couple of slugs at the fleeing riders but was more concerned right now with the fire. Reining to a sliding stop in front of the barn, he swung from the saddle and hit the ground running. Ducking through the open barn doorway, his gaze swept a look and landed on a bucket and some feed sacks.

Snatching them up, he ran to the watering trough just inside the corral, quickly dipped the sacks, and threw them to Jed and Homer as they dashed up. Scooping up a bucket of water, he ran toward the house as Tad and Mary rushed out the front door.

"Get some more buckets, Tad!" he screamed, as he threw his bucket of water on the leaping flames. Jed and Homer were frantically beating at the burning logs with their wet sacks.

For over an hour they fought the fire. Again and again they refilled their buckets from the horse trough and the water barrel on the front porch. Finally, only a few lingering tendrils of smoke puffed from the smoldering logs. The house had been saved and the Littlejohn family was safe. They were all exhausted as they collapsed under the shade of the big oak tree.

"Got any idea who those men were?" the sheriff asked.

"They said their names were Bob and Amos Dutton. The one Tad shot yesterday was their brother. Tad wounded the big man in the leg too," Mary told him.

"I see. Now it's all starting to make sense. I thought it looked like he was having trouble getting on his horse. I'm going after them," he said, pushing up onto his feet.

"I'm coming with you," Jed Holly said.

"Count me in too," Homer agreed, clamping his hat in place and rising. "Never did have any use for rustlers, much less for a man that would do harm to women and children."

"Can I come, Sheriff?" Tad called out as the three men headed toward their horses. I could ride one of the mules."

"I'd rather you stayed here, son, just in case they double back." George called over his shoulder. "Look after your folks. I'll be back."

Together, they watched the sheriff and their two neighbors ride away at a gallop.

"Thank heavens our family's safe," Mary breathed out loud, as she drew her children into her arms.

CHAPTER X

A loud banging on the front door jerked Doctor Lucien Robertson from sleep. He blinked himself awake and slipped quietly from the bed, trying not to wake his wife, although he knew it was no use. She was a light sleeper.

"Who in the world could that be at this time of night?" His wife asked. "It's almost midnight.

"I won't know until I go answer the door, dear," he replied gently. "Go on back to sleep. I hope Mrs. Johnson isn't having that baby yet, she's not due for another month.

"Nonsense, if it's a patient, you'll be needing help. Just let me slip my housecoat on and I'll be right in the office."

He had never gotten use to patients coming in the middle of the night, it always gave him a worrisome feeling, like the one he had in the pit of his stomach now. But he had sworn an oath thirty-one years ago never to turn anyone away that needed medical help, and he never had. Lighting the coal oil lamp and carrying it with him to the front door, he flipped the bolt and swung the door open.

Two strangers stood before him. One was an extremely large man. His face was whisker covered and he had evil looking eyes that were now glazed in semi-consciousness. A tourniquet was twisted tight just above a wound in his upper left leg but had failed to stem the flow. His entire pant leg was bloodsoaked clean down to his boot. A puddle had already formed on the porch where he stood. He seemed very weak and leaned heavily on a slimmer fellow whose darting eyes flicked a worried look up and down the street.

"My brother had a hunting accident," the slim man said. "He's got a bullet in his leg. You gotta take it out."

Lucien noted that last statement wasn't a request, it was an order.

"Bring him into my office, I'll take a look at it."

Lucien pointed to the examination table and busied himself unwrapping a bundle of sterile instruments and spreading them on a tray near the table. Lucille hurried into the office in her robe and with her graying hair done up in rollers. He didn't miss her appraising look that crawled over the two strangers, then the anxious look she sent his way, Lucille always worried needlessly. But this time he was worried too.

"I'll need some hot water, dear," he told her softly.

"There's still some in the kettle on the stove in the kitchen, I'll get it."

"Just hurry it up," the tall stranger said curtly. "We're in kind of a hurry."

Lucien didn't like the sound in the man's voice. He sure didn't like him talking to Lucille like that, didn't like it at all.

"Mister, I'm going to do everything I can for your brother, but you got no call using that tone of voice with my wife."

The man's eyes narrowed into a hard set. Anger ignited and flashed and boiled, molten, in their green depths, seemingly threatening to erupt in an act of unspeakable savagery at any instant. Then, as quickly as the mood had appeared, it disappeared and the stranger relaxed."Yeah, you're right, Doc. Reckon I'm just uptight about my brother."

Lucien continued to stare at the stranger, unable to shake the horror of what he had just seen in the man's eyes. Evil, he had seen the devil's evil in those eyes. A shiver of fear raced up his spine, he wished, oh how he wished he had never opened that door.

Lucille returned with a pan of steaming water and set it on a pullout shelf from the examination table. Taking up the scissors, Lucien slit the pant leg all the way up to the man's hip, then cut it off. Prying the bloody fabric loose, he removed it to expose the wound. Dipping a clean rag in the boiling water, he gingerly wiped the blood away.

He cleaned the wound with carbolic and cotton pads. The hole was a deep, dark red color and had begun turning an ugly shade of purple around the edges; it was a bad wound, but he had seen worse in his time. What worried him more than the wound was the amount of blood the man had lost; he had bled enough to kill a horse.

"Fetch me a bottle of laudanum from that cabinet over there, Lucille, I'm going to have to find that bullet and it's going to be painful."

"Will that stuff knock him out?" the tall man wanted to know.

"Well, he'll most likely pass out anyway from the pain and loss of blood. The medicine will just dull the pain some."

"Nope, no medicine. We've got to be moving on as soon as you get that bullet out."

"I'm afraid this man won't be able to go anywhere for several days. If he looses any more blood he'll die."

"You heard me, Doc. Just get it done!"

"Very well. You'll have to hold him down then, this isn't going to be easy."

"Nothing ever is," the man said, moving around to the head of the table and placing his hands on his brother's shoulders to hold him down.

Shaking his head, Lucien picked up the probe from the tray and slowly slid it into the wound. The giant let out a deep, guttural moan. Deeper and deeper Lucien inserted the instrument, following the torn canal made by the bullet. Using all his skill and experience, he probed the wound, searching for the slug. Finally he felt it. It had shattered the upper portion of the femur bone. It would be a long time before this fellow would walk again, if ever.

"Found it," he announced softly. "Lucille, hand me the forceps."

Slowly removing the probe, he replaced it with the long forceps, got a firm grip, and withdrew the heavy piece of lead. With a clink, he dropped it into the basin of water.

"Rifle bullet," he said softly.

"Yeah, like I said, a hunting accident."

Lucien cleaned the wound with a cottonball doused with alcohol, then wrapped the leg tightly with a bandage.

"He'll need to stay off that leg for a couple of weeks. That bullet shattered the bone."

"You saying he can't walk or ride?"

"If he does that wound will open up and he'll bleed to death or get infection, either way, it'll kill him."

"Well, Doc, I reckon that won't be no concern of yours," the tall man said, his words icy-cold, pregnant with deadly meaning.

Before Lucien could blink his eyes or react, in the space of two heartbeats, the tall stranger's hand flashed to the big Bowie knife in the sheath at his half-conscious brother's belt. Lamplight glinted off the blade of the big knife as it sped toward Lucien's stomach.

He felt his eyes wall white in disbelief. *Was this really happening?*

Then he felt it plunge deep, and slice upward. It burned like a red hot poker. He looked down. Horror swept over him. His stomach was open, gutted like a hog. His intestines were spilling out and stringing to the floor. He grabbed at them to hold them back. They felt wet and slimy and slithered past his clutching hands as weakness flooded his legs and he dropped to his knees in a puddle of his own insides.

A man's high-pitched hysterical laugh, a woman's bubbling scream!

His saddened gaze swung a searching look to find Lucille, and his heart shattered inside his chest. It was Lucille's voice! A prolonged wail of utter terror. The tall stranger was behind her. One hand held a handful of hair and jerked her head backwards. The other hand pulled the bloody blade across the beautiful softness of her neck.

Lucien closed his eyes...and shivered...and died.

A trail of blood made tracking easy. Sheriff Paxton and his two-man posse followed the two outlaws from Littlejohn's cabin until dark closed around them.

"What are we gonna do now, George?" Jed asked.

"Have you noticed they headed off to the west at first, then swung south? They're headed straight for town. Mary said Tad wounded that big fellow. I figure they're headed into town to get Doc Robertson to patch him up. Come on boys, let's burn some leather!"

They found Doctor Robertson and his wife, Lucille sometime after midnight. It was a gruesome sight. Homer Green took one look, grabbed his belly, and rushed outside but failed to make it before emptying his stomach. Jed Holly stood staring and cussing. Sheriff Paxton jerked two quilts off the bed and covered the bodies.

"Jed, Go wake up Marvin Tucker and tell him what happened. He'll need to take care of the bodies. Then wake up old Silas down at the livery. Tell him to see our horses are cared for, I'll be wanting them full and rested and ready to ride before first light. I aim to run them two jaspers into the ground."

Somehow word got around. Lamps were soon lit and the street was busy with milling and whispering townsfolk, wanting to do something, but not knowing what.

Before dawn, a dozen heavily armed riders sat their saddles in front of the Sheriff's office. George Paxton stepped from his office carrying his Stevens double-barrel shotgun.

"Before you boys decide if you want to ride with me there's a couple of things I want you to think about. First off, this ain't gonna be no Sunday school picnic. Some of you have asked how long we will be gone. The answer is I don't know. We'll be gone as long as it takes. I aim to catch these fellows come hell or high water. If you got obligations that can't wait, then you need to go back home.

"The men we're after are cold-blooded killers. Some of you saw or have heard what they done to Doc Robertson and Lucille. I just now met with the town council. They've put a five-hundred dollar reward on each of these fellows dead or alive.

"Those that want to ride with me, raise your right hand.

"Do you swear to uphold the laws of Lufkin County to the best of your ability? Say, I do."

A chorus of husky voices agreed.

"I hereby deputize you as a deputy sheriff of Lufkin County, Texas."

"I've hired Wolf-Cries-in-the-Night and one of his cousins to track for us. They're better at trailing men than all of us put together. They just told me the two men we're after headed northeast out of town. These fellows are unpredictable. No telling what they might do. They've already tried to burn down Littlejohn's house and murder his family. Jed, you and Homer, both of your places are out that direction. I want each of you to pick someone to go with you. Ride hell bent to your places. These fellows might try to pick up fresh mounts.

Taylor, I want you and Hensley to ride to Littlejohn's place. Be careful to let them know who you are before you ride in or that boy might shoot first and ask questions later. The rest of us will stick to their trail and try to run them down. Any questions? Then let's light a shuck, boys!"

Dawn streaked the eastern sky. Hooves crunched in the sandy street. Saddle leather creaked. Horses snorted. Little clouds of steam puffed from the horses' nostrils and were whisked away by a crispy October morning. Women clutched shawls or quilts about their shoulders and watched their men gallop away.

By mid-morning the Osage trackers picked up the blood trail. At first only a drop now and then but as the morning wore on, the drops became a steady trail. George knew it wouldn't be long now.

They found the big one lying between two big rocks, barely conscious. His left leg was bare and bloody. A Smith & Wesson lay in his lap. His horse was nowhere to be found. It was obvious his brother had left him here to die.

"What are we gonna do with him, Sheriff?" Someone asked.

"Take his pistol and knife and tie him to that tree over yonder. If he's still alive when we get back, we'll haul him back to town and hang him. Let's ride!"

All day they pushed their horses relentlessly. By sundown it became apparent they were losing ground. Their own horses were spent, while the outlaw was trading off between his two horses, riding one and resting the other. It became clear they would never catch him. He was headed straight for the Indian Territory. He had sacrificed his own brother in order to get away. As bad as he hated to do it the sheriff ordered the posse to turn around and head home.

Unbelievably, the giant was still alive when they got back to where they had left him. One of the men gave up his horse and rode double with another posse member so they could haul the killer back to town. If he lived through the fifty-mile trip, belly down across the saddle, Lufkin would have its very first hanging.

CHAPTER XI

*I*t's good to be home, T. J. thought as he and Lupe and their little caravan approached the outskirts of Lubbock. They had been riding hard for the past three days and both of them were worn out. Both they and the horses were covered with grimy layers of trail dust and sweat.

The thin morning sun had barely tilted westward. The main street of Lubbock was a beehive of activity. Heavy laden freight wagons, families in their farm wagons, men on horseback, and busy shoppers on foot hurried to wherever it was they were going told T. J. the day of the week must be Saturday.

A half-dozen howdies later he reined up in front of the sheriff's office and swung tiredly from his saddle, stomping feeling back into his numb feet as soon as they touched the ground. Swiping the hat from his head he slapped trail dust from his sleeves. George Paxton must have seen them through the window because he hurried out the door with a Texas size grin and hand extended in greeting.

"T. J., old friend, you are a sight for sore eyes," he said, his face split in a long smile and started pumping the offered hand like he was filling a water trough. "I've got lots of news to catch you up on, come on in and sit a spell."

"Been sitting for the most part of three weeks. George, say howdy to my friend, Lupe. He's going to be working with us out at the place."

"Good to meet you, Lupe," the sheriff said, swinging a look and sticking out a hand. "Any friend of T. J.'s is a friend of mine."

The boy took the hand and clasped it warmly, glancing quickly at T. J. as if searching for approval.

"Son, how about taking our horses and pack mule down to the livery? See they get fed, watered, and rubbed down good. I reckon they're might near as tired as we are. I'll be down directly."

"Yes sir," the boy said, gathering the reins and heading that direction.

"How was your trip?" the sheriff asked. "I already heard you got the Sanchez brothers. Nice work."

"It's a long, hot ride. We had a run-in with three Apache on the way back. They thought they wanted our stock. We convinced them otherwise."

A half-grin wrinkled George Paxton's face as he turned and headed inside the office. "Uh huh, I can just imagine. Grab a chair, T. J., I've got some bad news."

He tensed at the words. Wrinkled lines in his weathered face deepened and his eyes narrowed to thin slits. "What kind of bad news? Anything happen to my family?"

"Well, yes and no," the sheriff stuttered. I'm not exactly shore where to begin."

"Start at the start and don't leave nothing out, George. What's going on?"

* * *

The telling took awhile. Finally, he had related the events exactly as they had happened. T. J. sat silently until the sheriff was finished, a concerned look burning on his rugged face.

"This fellow you caught up with, is he still alive?"

"He's alive, barely. I still ain't sure he's gonna make it. Most men would have been dead and buried already but that jasper's as strong as an ox. Maybe its poetic justice that the only man in town that might save him is the one they murdered. Course, I don't reckon it matters a whole bunch. If I have anything to say about it, even if he recovers, he'll hang."

"Have you talked to him to find out where his brother might have hightailed it to?"

"He ain't in no shape to talk. He's awake, at least part of the time, but like I say, he's barely hanging on."

"I'd like to see him."

"Don't see it could do no harm I don't reckon. Course, you understand I'll have to ask you to leave your pistol out here, not that you'd do anything mind you, just the rules."

"I understand, George. I just want to have a looksee," he said, handing his pistol to his friend.

The sheriff took down a key from a wall peg and unlocked the heavy wooden door that led to the lockup. T. J. followed as they entered the narrow hallway that fronted the two cells. The prisoner was lying on the bunk in the first cell.

For a long minute T. J. stared. A flush swept through him. Anger festered. As he stared, the man's eyes slowly pried open, blinked, focused, and drifted over T. J. with open disdain. A look of pure murderous hatred saturated the man's eyes. They were the eyes of a man for whom death held no fear and possibly some pleasure. T. J. saw evil there. *This man tried to murder my family. He attacked and tried to burn down my house. If he don't die the law better hang him else I will.*

T. J. turned away abruptly.

"And you say my family's okay?"

"Yeah, they're fine. I was out there just yesterday. They shore are burning their eyes watching for you to get home though."

"I'm headed that way just as soon as I pick up a couple of things. I got me a bad case of the lonesomes. Thanks George," T. J. said, sticking out a hand. "I'm shore obliged for all you done."

"Don't mention it. You'd do the same for me. You've got a family most men just dream about having, T. J."

"Yeah, reckon I do."

"Oh, I plumb forgot to tell you. You're a famous fellow around these parts, T. J."

"Don't reckon I know what you're getting at."

"The story about you killing the Sanchez brothers and how you buffaloed that big rancher fellow has been plastered in all the newspapers. Folks been talking about it for a week."

"Well I'll be," T. J. said as he left the office shaking his head.

His next stop was at the Wells Fargo office.

"I'm T. J. Littlejohn," he told the young clerk at the desk. "I'm supposed to pick up something."

"Littlejohn? Oh! Yes, sir, Mr. Littlejohn. You'll need to talk to Mr. Thompson, the manager. Just a minute, I'll tell him you're here."

T. J. had seen the short, pudgy fellow that emerged from the back office around town a time or two, but had never actually met him. The man hurried toward him with a beaming look and an outstretched hand.

"So you're the man everybody's talking about. I want to shake you're hand. I'm Jacob Thompson. Come on in the office, I've got something that belongs to you."

"Reckon so," T. J. said.

"Why, the whole towns already heard what happened down at Alamogordo. How you blowed those killers to Kingdom Come and took that high and mighty rancher down off his high horse. You're a famous man around these parts."

"Don't know nothing about famous, just done what I had to do, nothing famous about that. I'm supposed to pick up some reward money, I believe."

"Yes sir, got the bank draft right here," he said, withdrawing a brown envelope from the safe. "I'm supposed to take a look at the signed affidavit from the Alamogordo officials, just a formality, you understand."

T. J. pulled the paper the Marshal in Alamogordo had given him from his pocket and handed it to the manager. The Wells Fargo man scanned it briefly and handed it back.

"Just take that over to the bank and they'll cash it for you. Mr. Littlejohn, it's a pleasure doing business with you."

"I reckon the pleasure is mine," T. J. said, waving the bank draft in the air before turning on his heels and striding from the office.

His next stop was the bank where he cashed the Wells Fargo draft and walked out with more cash money than he had ever held in his hands in his whole life, six hundred dollars.

Next, he went to the General Store. Wiley Stubblefield and his wife were both busy waiting on customers. Several shoppers were browsing around. The storekeeper glanced up. Recognition wrinkled his face in a big smile that tilted his mutton-chop mustache upward a notch or two.

"Howdy, T. J.," he said loudly. "When did you get back?"

"Just a little bit ago. I'll just look around till it's my turn."

T. J. couldn't help noticing the unnaturally friendly looks the other customers flashed his direction. It was a strange feeling. He wasn't use to that, usually people around town walked clear across the street just so they didn't have to meet him face-to-face.

Finally, Mrs. Stubblefield hurried over.

"I couldn't help noticing that you were looking at our ladies dresses. Is there something in particular you are looking for, Mr. Littlejohn?"

"Yes, ma'am. I'd like to pick out one for my wife and oldest daughter. It's been awhile since either of them had a new dress."

"That's wonderful. As a matter of fact, we just got a new shipment all the way from Dallas. I'm sure we can find something they would like. It's been over a year since I've seen your wife, but I believe this one would fit her nicely," she said, taking one from the rack. It was a shiny blue, the color of the sky on a bright summer day. Both the neck and sleeves were trimmed with white lace.

"Reckon that's the prettiest dress I ever laid eyes on," T. J. said, already deciding that was the one he wanted for his wife. "I need one for my daughter too. She's twelve going on twenty."

"As I recall, a beautiful young lady too. If I remember correctly, she has golden-blond hair like her mother, does she not?"

"Yes'm."

"What about something like this one?" She asked, selecting a white dress trimmed with yellow lace the color of sun kissed corn tassels. "I think this would look lovely on her."

T. J. bobbed his head once. "Shore is pretty."

"Now I need a doll, the prettiest one you got."

Mrs. Stubblefield smiled. "I know who that would be for. Her name is Sally isn't it? I have just the thing, and it even has blond hair."

While the storekeeper was figuring up his bill, including the credit he had extended T. J. earlier, he strolled back to look longingly at the picture of Mary's stove. *Shore would like to get that stove for Mary. Reckon I ought to? Guess I better not. They'll need the money worse than they'll need a fancy stove.*

With his wrapped packages tucked under his arm and the paid bill for Tad's rifle in his pocket, T. J. Littlejohn's steps were lighter as he strode toward the livery. Women he met smiled real friendly like. Men said howdy. And not one person veered out of their way to avoid him. *Something about all this shore seems strange,* he thought.

He found Lupe sitting on a bale of hay surrounded by a whole passel of German Shepherd puppies. Old Silas leaned against the corral fence in his leather apron watching the boy. He glanced up when T. J. approached and spit a long, thick stream of his ever present brown tobacco juice to his side.

"See you made it back all in one piece," the old timer said.

"Yep."

"Guess you know you're a famous fellow in these parts now?"

"Heard something about it."

"You mean you ain't seen that story in the newspaper?"

"Nope."

"Well sir, the story goes that the newspaper down in Alamogordo wrote about all that happened down there. Marvin Todd down at the Lubbock newspaper got wind of it and done some investigating. Then he put a big story in his paper about you. Seems the news people down in Dallas got wind of it and put it in their paper too. Now folks all over Texas are saying you're the greatest thing since churned butter."

"Well if that don't beat all," T. J. said, blowing out an exasperating sigh. "Reckon I better try to find one of them papers. Mary might get a kick out of reading about it."

"I saved a couple of copies. You can have one of mine if you want. Guess you heard about Doctor Robertson and Lucille?" the liveryman asked, shaking his head sadly. "Worst sight I ever seen."

"Yeah, I heard."

As they talked T. J. watched Lupe holding one of the puppies, softly rubbing its ears. The large oval eyes of the dog stared up at the boy. T. J. could have sworn he saw love reflected there.

"See your dog had a litter."

"Yeah. How many of 'em do you want?"

"What do you think, Lupe? Reckon you could find time to take care of that pup?"

The boy's dark eyes flashed and sparkled. His lips parted in a wide grin, showing his pearly-white teeth. "Yes sir! I sure could!"

"Then I reckon you got yourself a dog. Got any idea what you'll name him?"

"I think I will call him, 'Shep.'"

All day long Mary had felt an unexplainable excitement. Call it a woman's intuition, call it anticipation, but something inside her told her T. J. would be home today.

She busied herself in the kitchen. She had planned all day for the special supper. Tad had brought home a half-dozen fat fox squirrels from his latest hunting trip. A batch of fresh bread was rising and a fresh apple pie was cooling. She would make a pan of milk gravy, T. J.'s favorite meal.

The afternoon wasted away. She must have made a hundred trips to the front door to scan the horizon, each time fully expecting to see him riding over the distant hill. Each time the disappointment gnawed away at her self-assurance.

Suppertime came and went. Her heart sank. They ate in silence. Mary picked at her food. Her stomach was so queasy she couldn't eat. *How could I have been so wrong? The feeling was so strong.*

"Shore was a good meal, ma," Tad said around a mouthful of biscuit as he sopped the last drop of gravy from his plate with a pinch of bread. "Reckon that's about the best meal I ever ate."

His comments brought only a half-hearted smile. "That's exactly what your father would have said," she managed. "It's your father's favorite meal."

"Can I have a piece of apple pie now?" Sally asked excitedly. "I ate everything on my plate."

"Yes you may. Marilyn will cut you a piece, but just one, mind you, I want to have some left for your father when he gets home."

"When's papa coming home, mama?" Sally pressed, holding her plate while Marilyn cut the pie.

"He'll be..." her words drifted off like wisps of smoke on a still day. "I think I'll go sit on the porch for awhile."

Mary drew a shawl tight around her shoulders against the chill of a crisp fall evening and folded into T. J.'s rocking chair. The last glimpse of a blood-red sun filtered through tall pine trees on the western ridge and bathed the valley in a dusky glow. Earlier that morning she had watched its birth, throughout the day she had observed its life, and now she was witness to its death and burial somewhere beyond the distant horizon.

Maybe he's watching that same sunset, she thought. An overwhelming feeling of loneliness overtook her. *I was so sure it would be today.* Anxiety squirmed in the pit of her stomach, taut, twisting, and churning. Her eyes brimmed over with tears and scorched trails down her cheeks. She clutched the shawl in tight fists, weeping silently and closemouthed, her body shaking with spasms of hopelessness.

Again, she lifted her tear-blurred gaze to the sweeping hill across the creek and let it settle there, fixed, unblinking. Her throat tightened. Her eyes burned. Her heart ached.

She leaned her head against the back of the rocker and closed her eyes. *Oh God...we have so little time left together. Please don't allow it to be shortened further.*

Time crept slowly. Dusk settled in.

Maybe she heard something, maybe it was intuition, almost afraid to open her eyes lest it turn out to be only her imagination, and she breathed a silent prayer and looked.

Two riders appeared on the distant hillside. She squinted her eyes against the darkening dusk. An extra horse and a pack mule trailed behind the two riders. One of the riders rode a big buckskin. *T. J.!*

They were plowing through the creek. Even as she shot up out of the chair she saw him put his horse into a gallop, its long legs quickly closing the distance between them.

A happy scream burst from her throat amid sobbing laughter. Brimming with anticipation she flew off the porch and ran to meet him as fast as her feet would carry her.

The big buckskin sped toward her and she toward it on a collision course. T. J. vaulted from the saddle amid a sliding stop. He covered the remaining distance between them in long strides and scooped her up into his strong arms. Ignoring the rough stubble of his beard and the grime that covered his clothes, she smothered his face with kisses. Her hungry mouth found his. She curled an arm around his neck and held on tight.

He was home.

CHAPTER XII

It was late afternoon when Bob Dutton reached the Canadian River. He reined up sharply. For three days he had pushed himself and his two mounts relentlessly, stopping only occasionally for water and to catch a few minutes rest. He had lost one of the horses the day before, it had just stopped, stood spraddle-legged and refused to budge another step. He shot it between the eyes. The nag he now rode was on its last leg too; he had to find another horse.

Another days ride due north and he would be home. *Home.* The thought brought back memories, some good, most bad that he couldn't throw off. His pa had been a drunk and a man with a lot of hate bottled up inside and he had taken that hate out on everyone around him.

For as far back as Bob could remember his pa had sudden fits of anger when, for no apparent reason, he would take a notion to beat up on somebody. Usually his wife was the target of his violent outbursts but often all three boys too. That had all ended on Bob's twelfth birthday.

He didn't even remember what started it. It didn't matter. Everybody in the house had seen it coming, the sulking mood, swilling that homemade rotgut. Little Billy had said something pa didn't like and he backhanded him clear across the room. Ma knew better than to open her mouth but she did it anyway, and then he started in on her. He knocked her to the dirt floor of their little house then climbed astraddle her, grabbing a handful of hair in each hand and pounding her head against the hard-packed floor.

He didn't remember grabbing the old single-barreled shotgun. He didn't even remember using it like a club to knock pa off ma. But he remembered very well seeing his pa lying there on the floor, cowing like a whipped dog as Bob slowly and deliberately raised the gun and drew back the hammer. He remembered all the beatings, all the hurt, all the hate bottled up inside that felt like it would explode his belly if it didn't come out.

To this day he still remembered the feelings that swept over him when he pulled the trigger and watched his pa's face disappear, relief, freedom, and elation. For several minutes he had laughed hysterically, uncontrollably.

Too bad about Amos, he thought briefly. *It was his own fault though, he never was to smart. Hated to leave him like I did but we both couldn't make it. Besides, he was gonna die anyway, most likely he had already croaked before that posse found him. At least his horse helped me outrun that small town tin star and his men.*

He hadn't worried a whole lot about that Sheriff though, Bob Dutton knew enough about the law to know the posse couldn't chase him past the County line. The Texas Rangers were something else again. They would be after him like hounds on a fox's trail. He wanted to put as many tracks as he could between them and him. The lawless badlands of the Indian Territory where he grew up looked pretty good to him right now.

A slow sweeping gaze took in his surroundings and brought back memories of the times he had been here before. His eyes narrowed and the hint of a cruel smile curled one corner of his mouth as his gaze came to rest on the store, more importantly, the horses in the nearby corral. That would solve one of his problems. As soon as he got himself a new horse and crossed the river, the law couldn't touch him.

Coon's Trading Post stood on a rise on the Texas side overlooking the Canadian River. The river separated Texas and the Indian Territory, home of the Five Civilized Tribes, sometimes called The Nations. It was a lawless land where the gun a man wore and his skill at using it was the only law a fellow had to concern himself with, and that was just the way Bob Dutton liked it.

A large horseshoe-shaped bend slowed the river and created a natural crossing called Antelope Hills. Large herds of Texas cattle passed this way on their journey to the railheads in Missouri or Kansas. Antelope Hill Crossing was located about a mile upstream from the Post. The old trader made his living trading with drovers of the cattle herds, Indians, and men running from the law.

Jamming his spurs into the tired horse's sides, he headed for the store. Three horses stood hipshot in front of the store, their reins looped over the hitching rail. They had obviously been there awhile.

He eased his mount up to the watering trough and let it drink its fill. As he did, he eyed the broomtails in the corral and decided they weren't in much better shape than the one he was riding. He might just have to arrange to *borrow* one of those at the hitching rail. The red bay mare particularly appealed to him. It had a blaze face and four white stockings. It was by far the best of the lot. None of the three horses wore a brand.

Walking his horse to the rail, he tied it next to the bay. As he stepped up onto the narrow porch he lifted his pistol and settled it back into the holster loosely, then pushed through the door. He paused just inside the door to let his eyes adjust to the dim light.

He allowed his searching, unhurried gaze to sweep the narrow room.

Coon's Trading Post was like most every trading post he had seen in his time, only worse. The air inside the low-ceiling log structure hung thick and smoky and stank with the smell of stale whiskey, tobacco smoke, unwashed bodies, and raw hides of every description.

A big man with a whiskered face and shoulders a yard wide looked up from behind a long plank stretched between two barrels that served as a makeshift bar. The big fellow eyed Bob suspiciously. He figured it was Ben Coon himself.

Three cowboy types lounged around a dilapidated table sipping whiskey, most likely home grown. Judging from the way they slouched in their chairs it appeared all three had enjoyed way too much of Coon's rotgut.

"Whiskey," he said softly, fixing the barkeep with a stare. "None of that washtub slop either, understand?"

Coon opened his tobacco stained mouth to say something but obviously thinking better of it, reached into a small cabinet and withdrew a bottle of *real* whiskey.

"Jest passin' through?" The Big man asked in a raspy voice.

Bob touched the glass to his lips, threw back his head, and downed its contents in a single swallow before answering.

"Nope, I'm chasing a horse thief."

"Ye don't say? What kind of horse ye lookin' fer?"

"That blood-red bay mare outside. Somebody stole it from me about a week ago. Happen to know who's riding it?"

The natural wrinkles in Coon's forehead furrowed deeper and his bushy eyebrows dipped in doubt. His smoky eyes flicked to the three men sitting at the table.

"What was you saying, mister?" A young looking, sandy-haired cowboy spoke up loudly, his voice slurred by whiskey.

"You the fellow that's riding the bay?" Dutton asked.

"Yeah, what about it?" The cowboy asked, pushing unsteadily from his chair.

"That's my mare. You stole it about a week ago. I've been trailing you ever since."

"You're a liar! I raised that mare from a colt."

"And you're a horse thief," Dutton said, pulling his pistol. He drew it slow, almost casually, cocking back the hammer as he brought the gun up, and fired a little above hip level. The heavy slug drilled into the cowboy's chest and blossomed out the back of his shirt in a fine red spray. The impact knocked him back into his empty chair. The body jerked with false life.

Instinctively, his two companions leaped to their feet, clawing for their pistols. Dutton shot them both before their guns cleared leather. Standing there with his smoking pistol he let out a cruel laugh and twisted a look at Coon.

"Pour me another. You got a problem with me killing three horse thieves?"

"None of my affair," the trader said, his hand shaking so bad he missed the glass and spilled half the drink on the bar as he poured.

"Smart fellow," Bob said, spreading a thin smile. Picking up his drink, he walked over to stare down at one of the cowboys that was still alive. The man's chest wound emitted wet, sucking sounds. His eyes were walled white. Bright red foam dribbled from the corner of his mouth with every gasping breath.

"You look thirsty, cowboy. They say dying makes a fellow thirsty, I know killing does."

Lifting the glass, he slowly poured its contents into the dying man's face in a small stream as he emitted a cruel, open mouthed laugh. When the glass was empty he raised his other hand holding the pistol and calmly shot the man between the eyes.

* * *

A single candle flickered on a small table beside their bed. Shadows danced in the darkened room. Mary snuggled deeper into the recess of T. J.'s bare shoulder, her loose blonde hair cascading over his chest. The smell of freshly bathed skin filled her nostrils and love filled her heart.

Lifting her head she stared long at the man she had loved from the first moment she saw him. His eyes were closed but she knew he wasn't asleep. Inch by inch her slow gaze searched his face tenderly, studying it, memorizing it, loving it with her eyes. Where most saw only ugliness, she saw strength. Where some saw hardness, she saw gentleness. Where others saw evil, she saw character.

Her husband was a *half-breed*. To most people the word was spoken with distaste, even bitterness. T. J. was a man trapped in a No Man's Land between two cultures, not quite belonging in either, so he had withdrawn from both. She could understand why he had built a wall around himself and his family. She had witnessed the townspeople's intolerance. But for her, she felt she was the luckiest woman on the face of the earth.

She loved him and this valley and the life they had together. Her slow gaze crawled over him memorizing every detail, every line in his face. She wanted to store up every memory, every sensation because she understood as never before how precious each moment can be.

"It's so good to have my *famous* husband home," she teased, gently tracing a finger over his lips. "Did you miss me just a little bit?"

"No," he said softly, his eyes still closed, the word coming out in a raspy whisper. "I missed you a whole bunch. How about you, did you miss me?"

"I missed you every minute of every day," she told him softly. "I woke up every morning and reached for you and my heart hurt when you weren't there. I thought of you when I was sweeping or cooking supper or washing clothes and went to the door to look and see if you were coming. I lay in bed at night and cried myself to sleep because you weren't there beside me, yes I missed you, I'm glad you're home, and I love you so much."

"I love you too, Mary. You and the kids are what makes my life worth living. You're the best thing that's ever happened to me."

"Thank you for my dress, it's the most beautiful dress I have ever had. I'm going to wear it the next time we go to church. All the ladies will be envious. The children were thrilled to death with their presents too. Sally insisted on sleeping with her new doll."

"What do you think of Lupe?" he asked.

"He seems like a wonderful boy. He and Tad hit it off right away. They're both sleeping in the hayloft tonight, you know?"

"I think he'll be a big help around the place. That shore was a fine meal, maybe the best I ever ate."

Mary laughed. "That's exactly what Tad said. He's like you in so many ways."

"I reckon I've had happier days," T. J. said, "but I shore can't remember one."

"Then let's see if we can make tonight one you will never forget," she whispered softly against his lips.

Like a dewdrop settling on a soft rose petal her lips brushed his, tempting, teasing, tasting. Her fingers trailed along his cheek and gently touched his hair.

"I love you," she whispered, the full depth of her emotions wrapped up in those simple words.

He lifted his head and captured her mouth more fully, the hunger in his kiss filled her, ignited a fire deep inside her. She eased nearer, molding her body to his, feeling his warmth, his strength, his need. His palms splayed along her bare shoulder blades, gathering her, drawing her to him and holding her close.

Chill bumps danced across her skin. Her breath quickened

and went shuddery. Her body shivered with exquisite delight. Her blood pulsed in her veins. Her heart thundered in her chest. She could sense her energy building, blazing, flaming higher and hotter than she had ever known before.

Never had she loved him more than she did at this moment. Never had she needed him more.

The night was near spent. T. J. blinked himself awake but nothing moved except his eyelids. Mary lay with her head pillowed on his shoulder where it had been most of the night. Her arm stretched across his chest and her face tucked into the crook of his neck. He could hear her measured breathing and could feel her warm breath on his skin, her body touching his. He wished this moment would never end.

Outside a rooster crowed, announcing another day, a wonderful day, it was Sunday. The memory of last night brought a pleasant smile to his lips. *One thing for shore,* he thought. *She was right—it was a night I ain't likely to forget.*

It was mid-morning when they came. Tad saw them first and sounded the alarm.

"Wagons coming, Pa! Lots of them!"

T. J. looked up from greasing a wagon wheel and shielded his eyes from the sun. A line of wagons was topping the hill beyond the creek. He couldn't tell for sure from that distance but some seemed to be carrying lots of people while others appeared to be loaded high with lumber and such. *Reckon what's going on?*

Mary and Marilyn appeared in the doorway and stared at the strange procession.

"Who is it, T. J.?" she hollered. "Can you make them out?"

"Not yet. Shore a passel of them though. I count nine wagons in all."

Tad and Lupe scampered up on the corral fence to get a better look. The new puppy yelped and jumped at their feet. Sally leaped out of her swing, cradling her new doll in her arms, and ran to stand beside her mother. They all watched as the wagons rolled through the creek and up the near bank.

"That looks like Reverend Hensley in the lead wagon," Mary said in a puzzled voice. And that's Wiley and Doris Stubblefield from the store riding with him!

Wiping grease from his hands, T. J. walked over to stand beside his wife.

"Sheriff Paxton is the one on the horse riding alongside," he said. "Jed and Adelaide Holly is in that next wagon and that looks like Homer and Henrietta Green and their hired hand in that wagon after them...Mary, you got any notion what this is all about?"

"I haven't the slightest idea. Oh Heavens!" She exclaimed, patting at her hair. "Marilyn, does my hair look all right? Should I change dresses?"

"No mother, you look fine."

The line of wagons pulled to a halt a few yards from the house.

"Good Morning, T. J., Morning Mrs. Littlejohn," Reverend Hensley said, touching a thumb and finger to his flat-brimmed black hat.

"Morning, Preacher," T. J. said, still completely puzzled. "What's this all about?"

"Well, we heard about the fire and all and we understand from George you were planning on building another bedroom on the house come spring. We all got to talking about it and decided instead of just preaching about doing the Lord's work, it might be better to put some feet on our words. The long and short of it is, since it's the Lords day anyway..."

The reverend paused, stood to his feet, lifted his hat high into the air and shouted. *"We're here to have a house raising!"*

The folks in the wagons behind him stood and cheered. Mary cried and T. J. slipped an arm around her shoulders and tried to swallow the lump in his throat.

A two-man team used crosscut saws to fell long, lodgepole pines from the western ridge, while others used sharp double-blade axes to trim away the limbs. The logs were hooked to trace chains behind a team of mules. One man walked beside the team, handling the long reins and dragging the logs to the work area near the barn.

They were then cut to the needed length, stripped of all bark, notched and bored. A team of men used pry poles and ropes to roll the heavy logs up ramp poles into place on the growing wall. When in place, wooden pins were inserted into the bored holes and hammered home to secure the logs in place.

The women and older children were busy too. The boys carried water and mud from the creek while the women and girls mixed straw with the mud to form a special mixture. They sealed the wall by stuffing mud in cracks between the logs.

At mid-afternoon everybody stopped. The ladies spread two blankets together on the ground under the shade of the big oak tree. All of the women had brought their favorite dish: Fried chicken, roast beef, mashed potatoes, cooked turnips, and a dozen different kinds of pies. They set it on the blankets for a big picnic dinner on the ground.

Reverend Hensley raised his hand for quiet. A hush fell over the assembled crowd standing nearby.

"Folks, to my way of thinking, this is what being Christian is all about, neighbors helping neighbors. I'm reminded of the question a lawyer asked Jesus one time when he was trying to trip him up. 'Who is my neighbor?' the fellow asked. Our Lord answered the question by telling a story about a man that was robbed and beaten and left beside the road.

"Well sir, several upstanding folks in the community come along and saw the man lying there, but just kind of looked the other way and went on about their business because he was *different* from them. Then one fellow happened by and saw the poor man, picked him up, and helped him.

"Then Jesus turned to the lawyer and asked, 'Which one of these was a good neighbor?'

"Well, course the Lawyer had to say, 'The one that helped him.' Our Lord told him, 'You're shore right. Go and do likewise.' The good book calls the fellow that helped the other a 'Good Samaritan.'

"I reckon we've got a lot of 'Good Samaritans' gathered here today. To my way of thinking, we've already worshipped the good Lord more out here today than we could have back there in the church house in town, and I expect He is mighty pleased.

"Sermon's over. Thank you for all this good food, Lord. Amen. Let's eat!"

There was still an hour of sun left when they put the last wood shingle in place. Everyone was tired, but judging by the backslapping and smiling faces, it was a *good* tired.

T. J. stood beside Mary. His arm was wrapped around her shoulder. Amid the rattle of harness chains and the creak of wagon wheels, the last wagon turned into line and headed toward town. Both of them lifted an arm to wave goodbye. This had been a wonderful day.

CHAPTER XIII

"Pa, I just love my new bedroom," Marilyn said, as she helped clear the dishes from the breakfast table. She had just spent her first night in the newly constructed room.

"It's mine too!" Sally reminded her loudly.

"I know, but at least I don't have to sleep in the same room with Tad. He snores something awful!"

T. J. left Mary and the girls talking and moseyed outside. Tad and Lupe were busy slopping the hogs. He walked over, rested both elbows on the fence, and watched the boys until they finished.

"How'd you fellows feel about going for a ride?"

"Really?" Tad asked excitedly, flashing a grin that took up most of his face. "Wow, pa, we'd like that, wouldn't we Lupe?"

"Yes sir. Sure would."

Catching up their horses from the corral, they saddled them quickly, being careful to pull the cinch straps tight like T. J. had showed them.

"Should we take our rifles, pa?" Tad asked.

"In this country, don't never go nowhere without your rifle," he told them. "A fellow never knows when he's gonna need it."

He walked his buckskin up to the house and explained to Mary where they were going.

"We'll be back before noontime."

"Lunch will be ready," she told him, following him out to the porch. "You men folk be careful."

Both the boys beamed.

"How about showing me where those fellows had the stolen cattle pinned up?" T. J. asked his son.

"Yes sir," Tad replied, as he reined his sorrel around and struck a trot.

The boy seems older, like he grew a few years in just the few weeks I was gone, he thought, feeling a burst of pride swell in his chest.

They rode single file through the trees. Tad led the way and T. J. brought up the rear. Arriving at Short Mountain, the boy struck a small stream and followed it like he had been there a hundred times before. Breaking out of a thick stand of trees, the little spring fed valley lay before them. The rail fence was still intact except where they had pulled it down to let the cattle out. T. J. swept the sight with a slow turn of his head.

It was impressive. He had been there several times hunting, but had never really paid a whole lot of mind to it. *Might be a place to summer some cattle,* he thought, then it dawned on him, wasn't likely he'd be around come summer.

"Where were you when the fellow started shooting at you?" he asked.

"Right over there by that big rock. He missed the first shot and I was able to hunker down behind it."

"Where was the shooter?"

Tad pointed. "Up yonder on the side of that hill. See that pointed rock sticking up by that big pine tree? He was behind that."

T. J. squinted. His gaze measured the distance, deciding it had to be over a hundred yards.

"I hear you nailed him right between the eyes. That was quite a shot."

"You taught me, remember?"

"Appears you learned well. George tells me neither one of you would have got out of here alive if you hadn't done what you did. I'm proud of you, son."

"Thanks, pa."

"I haven't told your mother about this because I didn't want to worry her, but me and Lupe had a run-in with three Apache on the way back from New Mexico. They wanted our horses, most likely would have got them too, if it hadn't been for Lupe. One of them was about a heartbeat away from splitting my skull with his tomahawk when Lupe shot him. He saved my life. You boys are gonna make quite a team."

"I was scared so bad I about wet my britches," Lupe confessed. "Were you scared when you had to shoot that fellow, Tad?"

"Hate to admit it, but yeah I was."

"Nothing wrong with being scared," T. J. told them. "Any man that says he ain't scared when he's being shot at is a liar. It s nothing to be proud of, mind you, I've killed some men in my time but I never killed a man that wasn't trying to kill me. Sometimes a man has to kill to make it safe for those he loves. That's just the way of it.

"Son, I told Lupe about my sickness and that I only had a few more months to live. That's one reason I asked him to come live with us. You boys are gonna have to take care of the family after I'm gone."

Tad dropped his head with a hangdog look, suddenly studying the toes of his shoes. Lupe just stared, his brown face expressionless.

"Come on. I expect Mary's got lunch on the table. Then, we've got a lot of work to get done before sundown."

* * *

Amos Dutton was still alive. He lay on the bunk and listened as the heavy door at the end of the hall swung open. He had struggled back to consciousness just after sundown and was shocked to find himself locked in a jail cell.

For two hours or more he lay there thinking, trying to sort out scattered pieces of memory, and hurting, mostly hurting. His leg still hurt bad. Once he tried to raise himself up to look at it but the instant he tried to lift his head pain knifed through him and the blackness rushed back. He was too weak.

Everything was fuzzy and it hurt his head to think. He remembered getting shot at that half-breed's house. He remembered some riders coming and him and Bob having to hightail it. He remembered Bob helping him to the Doctor's office and the doc working on his leg. But after that everything got all mixed up. *How did I end up in here?*

The dim glow of a lantern cast a yellow circle of light in the darkened jail. He closed his eyes and lay motionless, not able to decide if he should play possum and pretend to still be unconscious or not. What good would it do? He was too weak even to lift his arm let alone think about escaping. He heard three sets of footsteps approach his cell. They stopped in front of the barred door.

"Looks like he's still out, Doctor. Want to wait until morning?"

"Sheriff, I come two hundred miles all the way from Dallas to doctor this fellow, don't see no reason to wait."

The key grated in the lock and the cell door swung open. Amos Dutton snapped open his eyes.

"Looks like he is awake after all," a short, stubby fellow said. He was bald headed except for a ring of snowwhite hair around the edges. He wore wire-rimmed glasses and a rumpled suit and carried a black doctor's bag.

Amos darted a look at the fellow beside him and recognized the sheriff, the one that had hauled in his kid brother across a saddle. A flush of hatred burned his insides and he struggled to bite off the words he wanted to say. A third man with a star on his shirt stood outside the bars.

"I'll be needing some hot water and clean rags, Sheriff," the doc said.

"Not shore I ought to leave you in here with this fellow, Doctor, he's a killer."

"Nonsense. I've rendered aid to lots of criminals. Besides, I doubt seriously if he would try to harm me. After all, I'm here to help him."

"Tell that to Doctor Robertson and his wife. This jasper and his brother gutted both of them like a hog after he had patched this man up. Keep a sharp eye Cecil," the sheriff said to the deputy. "If he makes a wrong move, shoot him, understand?"

"I'll handle it, Sheriff," the deputy said.

Did I hear him right? Amos's confused mind wondered. *Did the sheriff say we killed the doctor and his woman? I don't remember nothing like that, still, seems like I do recall something* Thinking so hard made his head hurt something awful.

The doctor cut away the bloody bandage that had dried and stuck to the wound. He gave the rag a final jerk to pull it loose. Amos gasped and let out a growl as a sharp pain shot through his whole body. He closed his eyes and gritted his teeth.

The sheriff returned with a pan of hot water and some rags. The doc cleaned and inspected his wound, grunting now and then.

"What do you think, doc?" the sheriff finally asked. "Is he gonna make it?"

"He'll pull through, at least unless that wound gets infected."

"Then I better tell the judge to go ahead and make plans for the trial. Folks hereabouts are fighting mad about what they done to Doctor Robertson and Lucille. They want something done and done fast."

"As much blood as this fellow's lost it'll take a few days before he will be fit to stand trial. I'll look in on him again tomorrow. See he gets plenty of food, that and rest will help him more than anything right now."

After the doctor left the sheriff and his deputy stayed around.

"I understand you're one of the Dutton brothers, Amos, ain't it?"

Amos rolled his head over to pin a look on the sheriff. "How'd you know who I was?"

"Well, for one thing your brother bragged about it out at the Littlejohn place when you tried to murder them and burn down their house. For another thing I found a wanted poster on you boys. It says you're all three wanted in Kansas for bank robbery and killing the bank clerk. Five hundred dollars reward on each of you."

"I ain't telling you nothin'!"

"Suit yourself. I figure that fellow we just buried out in boot hill was your younger brother. Am I right? Don't see how it could hurt to tell me his name so we could put a marker on his grave."

Amos thought for a long minute. His cloudy mind spun. His head hurt. *Billy outta have a name on his grave,* he reasoned. *Ma would want that.*

"Billy," he murmured. "His name was Billy Dutton. He was just nineteen."

"I'll see it's done," Sheriff Paxton told him. "The brother that run off and left you, Bob is his name ain't it, is he the oldest?"

"What you talking about? What do you mean, he run off and left me?"

"Just what I said. The reason he got away is because he took your horse so he could switch off and outrun us, your brother left you to get caught, or die, and he didn't give a hoot which."

"That's a lie!" Amos shouted, hot anger blazing in his face. "Bob wouldn't do that!"

"Well, you better think on this, you're fixing to go on trial for murder and will likely hang. He's long gone. Free as a breeze.

So you figure it out. Appears to me your brother is the sorriest pup of a bad litter," the sheriff said, then turned on his heels and slammed the cell door.

No witnesses! Bob Dutton reminded himself. That had always been his cardinal rule. True, Ben Coon had been accommodating, but refusing to leave anyone left around that could point an accusing finger at him had kept him out of jail for a lot of years. Dead men don't talk. *Oh well, I may as well finish my bowl of deer chili first, no use spoiling my supper.*

Bob's head bent low over the bowl, scooping the hot chili into his mouth. But his hard gaze pushed his eyelids up tight and was locked on the old trader pinning him with an unwavering stare. The man was clearly scared.

"This ain't half bad, Ben," Dutton murmured around a mouthful of the tart concoction. "How long you been running this post?"

"Goin' on three years," the man said nervously.

"Three years. That's shore a long time ain't it? I see a lot of stuff around here, you must be doing pretty good."

"Just a living."

"Is that right? That kind of surprises me. I mean, it takes a lot of money to buy all this stuff. Just look at that stack of hides, must be worth a pretty penny. Bet you sell a stack of hides like that once a year don't you, Ben?"

"What ye getting at, Mister."

"Bet you got a sack of gold double-eagles stashed around her someplace, don't you Ben?"

"Mister, if you got any notion of robbing me you're wasting your time. I ain't got two coins to rub together."

"Name's not, *Mister.* It's Bob Dutton. That name mean anything to you?"

"N...No. Should it?"

"Nope. Got any idea why you never heard my name before?"

"Don't know what ye'r getting at."

In one quick motion Bob swept his pistol out of its holster and shot the trader slap dab in the middle of his potbelly. The impact knocked him backwards against the shelf behind the bar, sending all the bottles crashing to the floor. Wiping chili from his mouth with a sleeve, Dutton rose and, stepping over one of the dead cowboys, walked casually over and stared down at Ben Coon.

"You ain't heard my name because I got a simple rule, Ben. I never leave witnesses."

Extending his pistol, he sighted along the barrel just like he had all those hours upon hours taking target practice as a youngster, only this time the *target* was the old trapper's eyes. After each shot he laughed hysterically.

Pouring himself another drink he sipped slowly and considered his next problem, finding the trappers money. He asked himself, *If I was Ben coon, where would I squirrel away my poke?*

With that thought in mind, he studied the room with a slow, searching gaze, absorbing every detail, searching every nook and cranny, alert for anything out of the ordinary. His eyes came to a halt in the very center of the square structure on the new looking potbellied stove. As far as he could tell, it, and the rock platform it sat upon, were the only recently added things in the whole place. The hard-packed dirt floor had been dug out so the rocks would be flush with the surrounding area.

Striding over, he dropped to his knees and inspected the platform closely. The dirt filled crack around one particular rock wasn't as smooth and hard-packed as the others. The old codger had been pretty clever, but not clever enough to fool a born thief like Bob Dutton. Withdrawing his Bowie knife, he used the point to pry up the rock.

Well, well, well. Would you look at this!

A hole had been dug in the ground underneath the flat rock. A small, leather, drawstring bag rested in the hole. Its contents bulged the bag's sides and their shape left little doubt as to their identity. The bag was full of double-eagle twenty dollar gold pieces.

Letting out an earsplitting yell followed by a long, high-pitched laugh, he fingered open the bag and poured the contents into his empty hand. The shiny coins filtered between his outstretched fingers and made a steady ringing sound as they hit.

Coming to himself, he decided he best be making tracks. He scooped up his newfound wealth, took time to empty the recently deceased's pockets, then fisted up two bottles of whiskey on his way out the door.

Stuffing everything in the saddlebag tied behind the fancy saddle on the bay mare, he toed a stirrup. Leaning over in the saddle, he untied the reins to the other two cowboy's mounts and gathered them in a fist. A *man can always use a couple of extra horses.*

CHAPTER XIV

"Think I'll ride into town this morning," T. J. said hoarsely over the rim of his coffee cup. "Anything by way of supplies you need me to pick up?"

Mary's fork stopped halfway to her mouth and just hung there motionless. She stared down at the table for a long moment without looking up or replying. She was afraid to put words to the thoughts that were in her mind. *Why is he going to town? Is he going away again?*

"Wiley Stubblefield was saying there's a new doctor coming from Dallas to take Doctor Robertson's place. Supposed to arrive yesterday. Thought I'd see if he'd take another look at my case."

His words ignited a small spark of hope inside her chest and stoked the smoldering coals to life again. She took a sharp breath in surprise and held it. Her eyes flicked up and found his, and held for a long moment.

"T. J.? Do you think...?"

Her unasked question was scattered with a shrug. "Don't know. Thought it couldn't do harm to ask."

Her heart leaped. A smile brightened her face.

"Well, there is something. The girls and I would like to make curtains for the window in their new bedroom. Do you suppose we could afford two yards of material?"

"Don't see why not. What color you ladies got in mind?"

"Pink," all three said at the same time. They all laughed. It was a happy moment.

"Pa, would it be all right if Lupe and I went for a ride after we get our chores done? Ma said it was okay with her if it was okay with you." Tad asked, still stuffing his cheeks with biscuit and sorghum molasses.

"Reckon so, but make shore the water barrel and trough are both full before you do, and don't get out of the valley."

"Yes, sir."

T. J. reined up in front of the sheriff's office well before noon and stepped down. He returned howdies from several passers-by and fingered his hat brim to a passing lady that smiled a greeting.

Sheriff Paxton looked up from a stack of important looking papers. He twisted his face into a grin, rose, and reached a hand across the desk.

"Morning, T. J., what brings you to town?"

"Thought I'd stop in on the new Doctor if he's made it yet."

"Shore has. His name is Tom Gattis—seems like a fine fellow. He set up shop in Doctor Robertson's old office for the time being. Glad to hear you're gonna let him look you over. How you feeling?"

"Tolerable."

"Glad you come in as a matter of fact. Take a gander at that," George said, withdrawing a wanted poster from a desk drawer and tossing it across the desk.

T. J. picked it up and scanned it for a time. His eyebrows wrinkled and he questioned the sheriff with a look.

"Seems there was already a reward on the Dutton brothers for bank robbery and murder up in Kansas. The Kansas folks are offering five hundred apiece for them. The town council put another five hundred apiece on Bob and Amos last week after they murdered Doctor Robertson and Lucille.

"We had a meeting last night. They voted unanimously that your boy deserved the reward for the younger Dutton brother he shot and also the thousand dollars for the one in yonder in the cell. They figure if Tad hadn't wounded him, we never would have caught him. I've already sent a wire to Kansas about the reward. Should be hearing back any time now, but the long and short of it is, Tad's got fifteen hundred dollars coming."

"Well if that don't beat all," T. J. said, shaking his head in amazement. "Seems he earned more reward money staying home than I did riding clear to New Mexico and back."

"He deserves it. If he hadn't done what he done likely your family or me either one would be here right now. He's a fine boy."

"He's shore growed up fast. It'll make him proud to learn about the reward."

"Yeah, thought the boy would be tickled about that. You can stop by the bank and pick the thousand up anytime. Soon as I get confirmation on the one from Kansas, I'll release that too."

"George, don't know who got that bunch together that come out to the house the other day but we're much obliged for all that was done."

"Can't say who got it started. Seems folks just started talking and one thing led to another. Don't matter. It got done. Everybody agreed we got more than we give. The preacher said that's how it always is."

"How's your prisoner?"

"The way he's eating, he'll be healthy as a horse in time for his trial. The judge set it to start next Monday, a week from today."

"He said anything about where his other brother might have headed?"

"Not a word. I told him how his brother took his horse and left him to get caught or die. He's stewing on that news right now. You thinking on going after the last one?"

"Yep. That fellow tried to do my family harm. He can't ride fast enough or far enough once I get an idea which way he's headed."

"I'll keep turning the screw on Amos and see if I can find out anything. We'll need Tad and Mary to testify at the trial, will that be a problem?"

"Don't reckon so. When will they need to be here?"

"Trial starts at nine sharp on Monday. Shouldn't last more'n a couple of days, if that."

"We'll be here. We're driving over to Homer Green's on Friday to help him and Jed Holly butcher hogs. You planning on being there?"

"Like to, but can't make it. I'll be getting things ready for the trial."

T. J. shook a nod and turned on his heel. "Be seeing you, George."

"Monday for shore," the sheriff hollered just before the door thudded shut behind T. J.'s back.

T. J. found the new doctor with a patient. He folded into a chair and waited, feeling a mite fidgety. The door to the office was open and he couldn't help overhearing the doctor and patient conversation. Listening curiously and judging the man by what he heard, T. J. decided right off he liked this new doctor. His voice was soft, gentle, and patient, but his words were spoken with authority, like a man that knew what he was talking about. Soon the woman patient left, casting T. J. a soft smile as she passed.

"Sorry to keep you waiting," the short, bald fellow said as he stepped into the hallway waiting room and fixed a look on T. J. "I'm Tom Gattis."

"I'm T. J. Littlejohn. Nice to make your acquaintance," he said, taking the doctor's offered hand and feeling a warm, firm handshake.

"I just got into town. Reckon I've got some mighty big shoes to fill. From all I hear, Doctor Robertson was a fine man."

"To my way of thinking, they don't get no better than Lucien Robertson and his wife."

"Come on into the office. What can I do for you today?"

"Well, truth is, Doctor Robertson examined me a while back and said I had something eating my insides. He said there wasn't anything he could do. Not that I'm doubting his finding, mind you, but I was just wondering if you might take another look?"

"Be glad to. You having any pain?"

"Some. It comes and goes. Feels like a knife jabbing me in the pit of my stomach."

"Passing any blood in your stool?" the doctor asked, lifting his gaze to T. J.'s face.

T. J. bobbed his head once in reply.

"From the looks of you, you've lost a lot of weight."

Again the doctor got a nod.

"Show me exactly where the pain is."

T. J. placed his hand just below his left rib cage. Doctor Gattis moved his own hand over the patient's stomach, pressing and probing.

"How's your appetite?"

"Mostly good. Sometimes I don't keep it down when I have a coughing spell."

"Any blood ever come up with it?"

"Now and then."

The doctor swiped off his spectacles and leaned back in his chair, nibbling at one of the earpieces and staring off into space in deep thought. For a long minute or two he said nothing. T. J. waited. Then, letting out a long sigh, he looked T. J. in the eyes.

"Mr. Littlejohn, from what I can see, I'm afraid Doctor Robertson's diagnosis was correct. I'd say you have a malignant tumor of the stomach. Someday, somebody will discover a cure for it, but right now, there's just not much we can do. I'm sorry."

T. J.'s features went stony. He looked down, studying the space between his boots for a long minute. He swallowed his disappointment and shuttered his feelings deep inside but it shore was a bellyful. When he looked up, his mouth was set in a tight line.

All the way home he tried to figure out how to tell Mary; it would be hard. Clearly she'd gotten her hopes up, now they would be shattered again.

It was dusky dark. Their valley was already cloaked in lengthening shadows. A thin tendril of smoke trailed upward against the gray sky from a waning supper fire. Apprehension swelled in T. J.'s stomach as he crossed the creek. Their new little German Shepherd puppy discovered his presence while he was still a good ways off and alerted those in the house with its loud, high-pitched yelping. The front door opened spilling a square of yellow light onto the porch. Both Tad and Lupe emerged carrying their rifles.

The sky was still the blackest black—the deep darkness that comes just before dawn. T. J. and the boys had the wagon hitched and waiting in front of the house. The boys' horses were saddled and standing nearby, swishing their long tails at pesky horseflies.

The black wash pot and extra wooden barrel were loaded in the wagon and the barrow they intended to butcher lay hog-tied in the wagon bed; the animal had finally stopped its earsplitting squeals.

Mary and Marilyn scurried around getting things together,

loading the supplies they would need for the big day, hog killing time at their neighbors. They spread a blanket behind the wagon seat for Sally.

The ride to Homer Green's place was a happy time. For awhile, at least, T. J.'s illness was, if not forgotten, at least pushed aside by the excitement of the day. Sally soon awoke and everything changed. Laughter and hurried conversations by the children were contagious; soon Mary and T. J. caught on, and the trip went quickly.

Tad and Lupe rode stirrup to stirrup. Both had been talking nonstop ever since they left the house, interrupted only by giggles and whispered comments.

"I think Tad must be telling Lupe all about the Holly's four daughters," Mary leaned over and told T. J. quietly.

"Most likely. It may be hard to keep their minds on their work with those girls around. You'll have to admit, though, Jed's girls are right pretty.

Mary cocked her head backward in a mock look of shock. "T. J. Littlejohn! I can't believe you said that!"

T. J. wrinkled a smile as Mary swatted him on the shoulder.

A thin line of gray smoke trailing upward greeted them long before they got within sight of the Green's home.

"Looks like Homer's already got a fire going heating water," T. J. commented, pointing with a nod of his head. "Reckon Adelaide will bring one of those wild plum cobblers of hers?"

"You know she will. She never misses an opportunity to show off. Wish I could ever learn to make mine taste like hers."

"In eighteen years you never heard me complaining about your cooking, have you?"

"No, but no one can make plum cobbler like Adelaide Holly."

"Maybe not," he whispered, leaning close so Marilyn and Sally couldn't hear. "But you make up for it in other areas."

His comment earned him one of those puckered-up smiles at

one corner of her mouth and a squeeze on his arm. "I'm so nervous about testifying in court Monday," she said. "Will that Dutton man be there?"

"I reckon so."

"I'll be scared to look at him."

"Then don't. Just look straight at me."

"But what if he says something to me?"

"They won't let him say nothing."

"What time do we have to be there?" she wanted to know.

"George said it starts at nine in the morning. I was wondering, what would you think about us driving into town Sunday morning in time for church? We could all stay in the hotel Sunday night."

"Oh, T. J.! Could we? I'd love for all of us to attend church together. That would be wonderful!" she said excitedly.

"Don't see why not."

"Did you hear that, Marilyn? Your father said we were going to church Sunday morning."

"Really? For sure?"

T. J. nodded a smile. "How's that hog doing back there, girls?" he called out.

"I think its dead, Pa," Sally said loudly. "He ain't moving."

"He *isn't* moving," Mary corrected, without turning her head.

"That's what I said," Sally agreed. "He ain't moving."

"Don't sass your mother," T. J. said in his sternest voice but with a sly grin.

"Yes sir, but I was just funnin' her."

T. J. cut a quick glance at his wife and saw her smiling happily.

As they drew near Homer Green's, it was clear they were the last to arrive, the place was a beehive of activity. Smoke lifted from under a large black wash pot filled to the brim with water. Nearby, a hole had been dug and a wooden barrel sunk deep at a slant. Above the barrel a tripod of sturdy poles held a rope and pulley.

"Howdy, folks!" Homer called as T. J. pulled his mules

to a stop.

Tad and Lupe reined up near the corral and began unsaddling. Homer's two boys hurried over to admire the new horses while all four of the Holly girls had their heads together admiring the boys.

"Where you want my barrow?" T. J. asked, climbing down from the wagon.

"Don't matter none," Homer told him. "If you want, just leave him be. Since you just brought one, if it's all right with you, we'll just go ahead and butcher him first."

"Morning, T. J., Jed Holly said, walking over.

"Morning, Jed. Looks like you fellows got everything about ready."

"Yeah, we'll get another fire going under your washpot. I'll get the boys started digging another hole to sink your barrel, that way we can keep one going while we clean the other one. Ought to speed things up a mite."

"How many hogs you butchering today?" T. J. asked.

"Five, all told, me and Homer's both got two apiece. Won't take long with all the help we got."

Marilyn and Sally had already jumped from the wagon and joined the Holly girls. T. J. helped Mary down.

"I heard that Dutton fellow's going on trial come Monday," Homer said, as he lifted the barrel from T. J.'s wagon.

"Yep," T. J. acknowledged.

"Reckon he'll hang?"

"I reckon."

"Would if I had anything to say about it," Jed added, helping T. J. unload the wash pot.

"How's the boy working out?" Jed asked, shaking a nod toward Lupe.

"Couldn't be better. He's a hard worker. Like one of the family already."

"Joshua," Homer hollered. "You and Caleb get some shovels

and get another hole dug for this barrel."

"Yes, sir," the boys answered, turning and trotting to do their father's bidding.

T. J. walked over to where Tad and Lupe were just turning their horses into the small split rail corral.

"You boys unhitch the team and turn them in the corral too, then start drawing water to fill our wash pot. I want both of you to pay close attention to what all goes on today. Learn everything you can. If you see something you don't understand, ask. It'll fall on you to do it all come next year."

"Yes, sir," they both said.

Working together, the men and boys made short work of completing the second hole and slanting the barrel halfway. The second wash pot was full and heating. Steam drifted upward from the first pot of water.

"Reckon the water's about ready?" Jed asked.

"Homer's the expert on that," T. J. said as all the men and boys gathered around.

"Boys, when it comes to butchering hogs, ain't nothing more important than the water temperature." Homer said. "If you get it too hot it'll make the skin come off. On the other hand, if it ain't hot enough it won't loosen the hair and makes it hard to scrape."

"How do you tell when it's hot enough, pa?" Caleb spoke up.

Homer Green coupled two fingers and dragged them backward through the water quickly.

"Now you boys do what I done."

One after another all the boys stepped forward and imitated him.

"That water's just about ready, but not quite. We want it just before it starts to boil. Put another couple of sticks under the pot there and let's add the ashes."

Homer scooped a shovel full of the gray ashes from the fire and dumped them into the pot of hot water and stirred them up.

"What's that for, Mr. Green?" Tad asked.

"My pa taught me that little trick when I was just about your age. Something about the lime in the ashes that makes the hair turn loose, makes it lots easier to scrape off. T. J., let's get your barrow over here. By the time we get him knocked in the head, bled and gutted, our water ought to be just about right."

For the next few hours everyone was too busy to hardly look up. One after the other the hogs were killed, bled, gutted, sloshed up and down in the hot water in the barrels, then scraped and butchered.

Everyone had a job: The boys were kept busy stoking the fires, drawing and heating water, and helping manhandle the big hogs from one location to another in the process. It was the women and girls' job to scrape the hogs, grind the sausage, and pickle the feet in vinegar.

All three men were well experienced at cutting up hogs, having been taught by their fathers just as they were now teaching their own sons. After the hogs were cut up, the meat was hung in the smokehouse to cure in the thick hickory smoke.

It was mid-afternoon before they finished. Five hogs had been processed. Three families would have meat aplenty to last through the long winter.

While the men and boys all trooped to the creek to wash up, the ladies spread dinner on a quilt under a tree. Fried fresh ham, sweet turnips, beans, cornbread, and even Adelaide Holly's plum cobbler quickly disappeared as the hungry crew enjoyed a happy meal.

It was a tired bunch of folks that said their good-byes.

"It's been a good day, T. J." Mary said, leaning her head against his shoulder as he headed the team and wagon into the sun toward home.

CHAPTER XV

Reverend Hensley was leading the singing when the door opened and the Littlejohn family entered. The preacher's booming voice suddenly trailed off in mid-sentence. A huge smile of recognition and elation spread across his face before he caught himself and resumed the song with even more gusto than before. Every eye in the building followed the pastor's gaze. The arrival of T. J. and his family, so long absent from any social event, caused quite a stir. They hurried quietly to the only empty pew in the whole room, the one nearest the front. The song ended before T. J. could get his family seated.

"We're mighty glad to have the Littlejohn family with us today," the pastor said happily, as hands from the pew behind them patted welcomes on their shoulders. "Let's all lift our voices in praise as we sing, '*Amazing Grace*'."

It seemed everybody in the church knew the words except him. He had never attended church until he met Mary, and only a few times since. Driving twenty miles to church just hadn't seemed practical to T. J., at least until now. He glanced quickly at Mary.

His wife's face was beaming. Listening to her as she sang, he realized for the first time in eighteen years just how beautiful her voice was. He stared at her, unable to tear his gaze away. Her beauty sent shivers over him. A lump crawled up the back of his throat.

The song ended and the preacher read from the bible. T. J. tried to listen to the words, but his mind whirled through a maze of thoughts: *Why didn't I bring Mary and the kids to church more? I didn't realize how much it meant to her. What will happen to her after I'm gone? Should I try to sell our place and move into town? I'll mention it to her and see what she thinks.*

Sally began to squirm between him and Mary. She was getting restless. A soft touch from Mary's hand quieted her.

Reckon how the trial will go tomorrow? Hope Judge Pennington don't let that Dutton fellow off. George said the judge seemed to have a burr under his saddle about sentencing a man to hang, most likely one of those do-gooders that thinks everybody can be turned from bad to good if you just try harder to understand them.

Hope George was able get a lead about where the other brother was headed. I need to get on the trail while I'm still able. Seems I'm doing some better though, at least I ain't had a bad coughing spell in might near a week.

Flicking a quick glance down the pew at the boys, a thin grin wrinkled the corner of T. J.'s mouth. They seemed more interested in sneaking peeks over their shoulder at the Holly girls than they were listening to the preacher, *but then, I'm shore one to talk, I ain't hardly heard a word he's said.* A feeling of guilt swept over him and he made a special effort to focus his mind on what Reverend Hensley was saying.

"And so, brothers and sisters, if you find your road of life is a mite rough lately. If you're going through a dark valley this morning and old Satan has knocked you for a loop, take comfort in knowing that Jesus is right there beside you. He has promised that He will never leave us nor forsake us. He'll pick you up, dust you off and lead you through the darkness and into the light of a new day. Amen!"

The preacher hurried down the isle to the front door where he stood to greet and shake hands with the worshippers as they filed out.

"Real good to see you and your family here today," Wiley Stubblefield said, leaning over the pew to shake T. J.'s hand and pat him on the shoulder. "Real fine message Brother Hensley brought, wasn't it?"

"Uh, yeah. It shore was."

"Morning, T. J." Jed Holly greeted as he walked up and stuck out a hand.

"Howdy, Jed. How's the hog smoking coming along?"

"Mighty fine. Your meat'll be cured out in a day or two and ready anytime you want to pick it up."

"Likely be the middle of the week. We'll be tied up with the trial and all 'till then."

"No hurry. Say, Adelaide brought a picnic lunch and wanted me to ask you folks if you'd share it with us down by the creek?"

"Yes, please do," Adelaide spoke up happily. "We could have a nice picnic on that grassy spot down by the bridge."

"Well, it's up to Mary. We're all staying in town at the hotel tonight so we will be here tomorrow in time for the trial."

"Only if you're sure you have enough," Mary said. "Six more mouths is a lot to feed."

"I insist. We'll have plenty," Adelaide Holly assured them, taking Mary by the arm. "Besides, the truth of the matter is, the girls did most of it. When they learned those boys of yours would be here today, nothing would have it except that we invite your family to join us for a picnic. Come on, let's go get stuff together. The men folk can come when they get through visiting."

"Right good message, preacher," T. J. said, shaking the Reverend's hand as he and several of the men made their way to the door.

"Sure was good to have your family today, T. J. Hope you will do it again."

"We'll make it a point to."

"Nothing would make me happier," the preacher said, still pumping T. J.'s hand.

"Howdy T. J.," George Paxton said, joining the wad of men gathering in the churchyard. "Good day, ladies," he said, nodding his head to the women folk as they hurried past.

"Everything ready for the big trial tomorrow, Sheriff?" Jed asked.

"Ready as we could ever be, I reckon. The Judge brought in a special Prosecuting Attorney and defense lawyer all the way from Dallas. He said he wanted to make sure the defendant got a fair trial. You're on the jury ain't you, Wiley?"

"Yeah, me, Silas Isaacs, Sam Moffet that's got that little farm north of town, Jacob Thompson, the Manager of Wells Fargo, Mel Black that owns the hotel, and Clay Douglas. Any of you fellows know him? He's the foreman of that new Triple-S ranch that moved in a few miles west of town."

"Don't reckon I know him," Jed said, shaking his head.

"He seems like a right nice sort of fellow," the sheriff told them. "If I'm judging him right, he can be tough as nails, but he talks real quiet. Nothing like any foreman I ever met."

"As long as he's a fair thinking man I got no gripe with him," Jed commented.

"I reckon he's that, all right," the storekeeper told them.

"George, you gonna be around your office later on this

afternoon?" T. J. asked the sheriff. "Thought I'd stop by and chew the fat for a few minutes."

"Deputy Mason is watching the prisoner today, but I'll have to relieve him for supper about five or so, will that be okay?"

"Five will be just fine."

"T. J., I reckon we better be moseying on down toward the creek if we expect to get any of that fried chicken I smelled them cooking early this morning," Jed told him.

"How come the rest of us didn't get invited to the picnic?" the sheriff wanted to know, glancing around the group of men with a questioning look and a grin on his face.

"If you want to know the truth of the matter," Jed informed them, smiling as he said it. "I think T. J. owes a thank you to those two boys of his that he even got invited."

It was a happy time, one of those times that etches itself in one's memory. The afternoon was nearly spent. They sat on a quilt under the shade of a big oak tree near the creek. The remains of their picnic lunch, though precious little after four adults and eight hungry youngsters ate their fill, still lay on a spread tablecloth nearby.

T. J. leaned his back against the tree and leisurely chewed on a grass stem. Jed Holly smoked his ever present pipe, the sweet aroma filling the afternoon air.

Laughter, good food, and a feeling of, *what is it?* T. J. tried to figure out in his mind, *acceptance, that's it! For the first time in my whole life I feel accepted by somebody besides my own family.*

"It's good to see the kids having a good time, isn't it?" Adelaide said.

"Indeed it is," Mary agreed, swinging a look at the circle of young people playing 'drop the handkerchief.' "Children need friends other than their own family."

"So do grown-ups" Adelaide said with a smile, and pushing to her feet added, "this has been so nice. Let's do it again."

"I'd really like that."

"Reckon we best be getting loaded up and headed home, wife," Jed said. "It'll be dark now by the time we get there."

"We'll be needing three rooms."

"You folks staying in town for the big trial tomorrow?" the hotel desk clerk asked.

"Yep," T. J. said as he signed the registration book.

"If you'll be needing rooms for the hanging better go ahead and rent them now, I'm expecting to be plumb full. We ain't had a hanging round here in a coon's age."

"Don't reckon we'll be coming for that," T. J. told him, taking the offered keys and motioning his family toward the stairs.

Mary flicked a happy glance his way as they made their way up to their rooms.

"Me and your mother will take room number one. Marilyn, you and Sally take number two and the boys will be in number three."

He pushed open the door and stood aside. A feeling of pride washed over him as he watched his wife step inside the room and look around. Her face was flushed with excitement.

"T. J., do you realize this is the first time I have ever stayed in a hotel?" Mary hurried to the bed and sat down on the edge, bouncing playfully and smiling broadly. "I'm going to enjoy sleeping in a strange bed tonight."

"Then I'd say it's about time," he said, walking over and pushing aside the curtain and gazing down into the street. "I'm going to walk down to the Sheriff's office and talk to George. You and the children rest easy for awhile. When I get back we'll have supper down at the café."

She rose to her feet and closed the space between them with a few quick strides. Her arms circled his neck and her head nuzzled against his chest. No words were spoken between them. None were needed. The love that radiated between them said what words could never say.

The door to their room thudded shut behind him and he dismounted the stairs two at a time. Mary's excitement gave him a good feeling; he enjoyed seeing her happy. No one was in the lobby as his long strides carried him to the front door. The streets were empty but after all, it was Sunday afternoon.

As he stepped off the porch a sharp pain in his lower stomach doubled him over. A deep, racking cough brought red liquid spewing from his mouth. Stumbling blindly, he managed to make it around the corner of the hotel into the small alley before collapsing to his knees. Surge after surge came up coloring the sandy soil in front of him dark red. With each upheaval his strength left him and he collapsed onto his side.

The buildings around him spun crazily. Spasms of pain wracked his body. The light was fading. *Am I dying? I didn't even get to say goodbye.* His thoughts faded as a deep velvety darkness wrapped its cloak around him.

CHAPTER XVI

T he ride from Antelope Hills had been uneventful. Bob Dutton felt good. He had a pocket full of money, without a doubt the best horse he had ever forked under his legs, and two more on a lead rope trailing behind. Life was good.

It was coming up on sundown when he rode up the overgrown trail and reined up in front of the ramshackle hovel he used to call home. *What a dump,* he thought, wagging his head in disgust. *Bet the rats have already abandoned this place.*

Swinging a sweeping gaze he surveyed the surroundings with a turn of his head. *Barn's still standing. Corral's got several rails down but ought to hold the horses. Graveyard's gown up where Ma's buried.* He swung a leg over the rump of his new bay and stepped to the ground.

He took his time unsaddling his horses and turning them into the corral. He propped some fallen rails up temporarily to keep them inside. Stashing the saddles in the dilapidated barn, he slung his new saddlebags over a shoulder and headed for the house.

Careful to avoid the busted planks in the small front porch, he pushed the squeaky door open with a hand.. *Same old rough plank table he'd ate at most every day of his life. Old potbelly stove in one corner. Ma's broken rocking chair lying on its side.* Bending down, he picked up part of a broken plate that had once been his Ma's most prized possession. Shaking his head sadly, he pitched it casually into a pile of trash in a far corner.

Memories flooded his mind as his gaze crawled slowly over the room. Pa's razor strap still hung on a nail beside the stove. *How many beatings have I received with that strap? Way too many. Since I turned twelve no man has raised a hand to me and lived to tell about it.*

Well, this will have to do for awhile. I'll lay low and let things cool off for a bit but I ain't gonna hang around this rat hole long. Them two bottles in my saddlebags won't last more'n a few days anyway. May Belle over at Enid will be glad to see me now that I've got some jingle in my pockets. Can't wait to get my hands on that little gal again.

"You can go get some supper, Cecil," the sheriff said as he walked into the office and hung his hat on a peg beside the front door. "Everything okay here?"

"Yeah, the prisoner is quiet until I look in on him, then he sets in cussing a blue streak"

"Stop by the café and bring a plate for him when you come back. Maybe some grub will quieten him down."

"I doubt it. That fellow's got the foulest mouth I ever heard on a man."

Lifting the keys from a nail, George unlocked the door to the jail hallway and walked inside. A half-dozen steps carried him to the cell where Amos Dutton stood gazing out the tiny barred window.

"Looks different from the inside looking out, don't it?" the sheriff asked.

"Yeah, you better not sleep too sound, lawman. My brother will bust me outta this dump."

"Your *brother* is likely laid up with some whore sipping whiskey and having a gay old time. You really think he's gonna risk his hide coming back here? You got an awful short memory. You're forgetting he run off with your horse and left you to die or get caught just so he could get away. He don't give a lick what happens to you."

"That's a lie. My brother wouldn't do that. Us Duttons take care of their own."

"Yeah, you just keep telling yourself that when the hangman slips that noose over your head. You ever see a man hang? Sometimes, when the hangman don't do it just right, it takes a long time. I've seen their eyes bulge right out of their sockets. Their tongue lolls out like a winded horse. Their lips turn purple and their feet kick the air until they slowly choke to death. Is that the way you want to die, Amos?

"Your trial starts in the morning. I expect the jury won't take more than a few minutes to find you guilty and the judge sentences you to hang. It might go easier on you if you'd tell me where that brother of yours was headed."

"Whatta you mean it might go easier on me?"

"Well, if you help me I'll put in a good word for you. I'll tell the judge you're cooperating with us and trying to help us find your brother. It most likely was him that killed the doctor anyway wasn't it?"

"I don't know. I don't remember what happened."

"See, that's what I mean. You were probably passed out from losing all that blood. Your brother likely done the killing and you're gonna hang for it. That don't seem fair to me, does it to you?"

"Ain't fair."

"Amos, if you're gonna help yourself here you best start telling me something I want to hear. It'll be too late after the trial starts."

Amos Dutton stared at the floor for a long minute. The sheriff waited silently.

"Suppose I was to tell you. What would happen to me?"

"Ain't no way of knowing for shore. The judge might be inclined to go easy on you if I could tell him you helped us find your murdering brother. I ain't promising nothing you understand, but you might end up just getting a few years in prison. Take my word for it, that would be a sight better than hanging."

"Bob shouldn't ought to have run off and left me like that, it ain't right. That ain't no way to treat his own brother."

"Not to my way of thinking it ain't," the sheriff agreed.

"He's headed for our home place up in the Territory."

"Where might that be?"

"On the North Canadian River 'bout a hard day's ride northeast of Antelope Hills on the South Canadian. It's where we was raised. Bob's got a bargirl he's sweet on over in Enid at a saloon called the Lucky Lady. Her name's May Belle."

"You done the right thing, Amos. I'll see what I can do to help you. Supper will be here in a bit."

George turned on his heels and walked back into the office, locking the door behind him. A thin grin of satisfaction wrinkled his features as he sat down to make a note of the information he had just learned. His writing was interrupted when Deputy Mason burst through the door all out of breath.

"Come quick, Sheriff, its Mr. Littlejohn. Somebody found him in the alley beside the hotel. He's over at the Doc's now. He looks plumb awful!"

"Hurry over to the hotel and bring Mary Littlejohn to the Doc's!" the sheriff ordered, grabbing his hat as he rushed out the door and trotted down the street.

T. J was lying on the examining table when George hurried in. "How is he, Doc?"

"Not good, I'm afraid. He's vomited up a lot of blood. That and the extreme pain he must have been going through caused him to lose consciousness. I think he'll come around in a few minutes. I just finished cleaning him up as best I could. He's a sick man."

"Yeah I know, but I guess I didn't realize just how sick. They were staying over at the hotel. His wife will be here any minute."

"I'm sure she's aware of his condition, isn't she?"

"Yes, I'm sure he's told her. To most folks he's not much of a talker, but he loves Mary more than life itself. He's told me as much more than a few times."

Mary rushed into the room followed closely by the deputy. A worried look occupied her face. Tear moistened eyes locked on her husband as she hurried to his side and lifted a hand to hold it to her chest. "What happened?" she asked anxiously.

"Someone found him unconscious in the alley beside the hotel," George told her.

"Is he...is he going to be all right? He looks so pale."

"Like I told the sheriff," Doctor Gattis said softly, "he's lost a lot of blood. I suspect it was the pain that rendered him unconscious. He's a strong man though. I gave him some medicine and I expect he'll be coming around pretty quick. He'll need some bed rest for a couple of days."

Coming awake took awhile.

Finally, after long, agonizing minutes, T. J. blinked.

"Where am I? What happened?"

"It's all right, T. J.," Mary said soothingly, bending to touch her cheek to his. "You just passed out for awhile from the pain and loss of blood. The doctor says you'll need some rest but you'll be up in a day or two."

"If it's all right, Mary, I'll get a few of the boys to help get him over to the hotel and into bed."

"Thank you George, I'd be obliged."

"I'll look in on him in the morning," Doctor Gattis said. "Meanwhile, give his stomach tonight to settle then see if you can get some soup down him in the morning. It'll help him regain his strength."

"I'll see to it, Doctor."

The long night seemed like forever. Morning broke cold and wet and a northern wind whistled outside. Dawn seeped slowly through the window and shaded their tiny hotel room in a gradually lightening grayness. T. J. was aware of these things but continued to stare wide-eyed at the ceiling, mind whirling, as he had done most of the night. He knew he was getting worse, and fast.

Hope George is able to get a lead on where that other Dutton fellow might be holed up, if I'm gonna have a chance of going after him I better do it pretty quick. Winter's coming on. The weather up in The Territory will likely be turning bad. Don't know how much longer I'm gonna be able to hold out. Shore would like to have that extra money to leave Mary and the kids though. With the reward from Kansas and what the town council put up, that would be another thousand dollars. That would go a long way toward taking care of Mary and the kids.

Mary's regular breathing told him she was still asleep. Her head lay pillowed on his shoulder, the way she usually slept. Her face turned into the warm, whiskery crook of his neck and her breath warmed his chest. He liked to listen to her sleep. The steady throb of her heartbeat melded with his. He could feel her soft body snuggled against him. Her nearness set off ripples of awareness in him just as it always did.

Folks look for happiness all their life, he thought, *and most never do find it. I reckon I've been luckier than most. Happiness ought not depend on how long it is, but how good it is, and I've had the best this old world has to offer but I shore do hate to leave her. Death. It seems so final. Am I ready for it, don't reckon*

I got a choice in the matter. He chewed on that thought for a time, lost in his spiraling thoughts.

A commotion down in the street scattered his thoughts. Shouting, running, horses galloping here and there didn't sound like a typical early morning in Lubbock. *Wonder what's going on?* His curiosity begged him to slip out of bed and see what was happening, but Mary was sleeping so peacefully he decided not to move. Besides, she would likely give him *down the river* if she caught him out of bed.

A loud knock on the door to their room jerked Mary to a sitting position. "Who could that be?" she whispered. "Surely it wouldn't be one of the kids."

"Who is it?" T. J. called out.

"It's me, T. J., George Paxton. I need to talk to you."

"You stay in bed," Mary instructed with a stern look. "I'll let him in."

Sleeving into her housecoat and tying the sash at the waist, she padded barefooted to the door and opened it.

An embarrassed look swept across the sheriff's face and he turned beet red. He stared open-mouthed at Mary for a moment before sweeping his hat from his head and diverting his gaze to the floor.

"I...I'm sorry, Mrs. Littlejohn, ma'am. I...hated to disturb you."

"Come on in, George. What is it?" T. J. interrupted. "What's going on down in the street?"

"Afraid I got some bad news. Amos Dutton escaped sometime last night. Somehow got his hands on Cecil Mason, my deputy. Broke his neck and got his keys and pistol. He pistol whipped old Silas near half to death down at the livery and stole that pinto that belongs to Lupe. Doc says Silas is in bad shape but ought to pull through. We're putting together a posse. Not sure how much start he's got on us but we'll do everything we can to catch him before he gets across the line. Thought you'd want to know."

"I'm going with you," T. J. said, throwing back the covers.

"That's not a good idea," the sheriff told him. "You ain't in no shape to ride. You best stay right where you are and get your strength back. The Doctor would have a fit. Besides, to be honest with you, chances of catching him before he gets out of the county are mighty slim."

"Please T. J.," Mary said, putting a hand on his shoulder. "Listen to George."

As T. J. touched his bare feet to the floor and tried to stand the room started spinning and his knees went soft. As bad as he hated to admit it, they were right. He sat back down on the bed.

"I'll drop by just as soon as we get back and let you know what happened," the sheriff told his friend as he clamped his hat on and turned for the door.

"Since there won't be a trial we'll likely start for home later this morning," T. J. said. "Be careful, George, that fellow's a bad one."

Amos Dutton hunkered lower in the saddle and clutched the collar of his coat tighter around his neck against the icy-cold north wind. His leg hurt something awful but he was so happy to be out of jail that he ignored the pain. *That tinhorn sheriff won't catch me this time, no siree,* he thought as he lashed out cruelly with the reins, urging the stolen pinto to greater speed.

Bob would be proud of me the way I fooled that deputy into getting close enough to get my hands on him. His neck sounded like a dry stick when it cracked..

Amos was still fightin' mad about the way his brother had run off and left him like he did. *I still might just kill him when I see him. I ain't decided yet.*

* * *

"Rider coming, Pa," Tad hollered from the woodpile where he and Lupe were laying in wood for winter. "Looks like Sheriff Paxton."

T. J. stepped out onto the porch and squinted over the rim of his coffee cup into the sun's glare. He watched his friend as he neared the house. *He looks tired.*

"Afternoon, George. Climb down and have a cup of coffee. You look plumb tuckered out."

"Don't mind if I do. How you feeling?"

"I'm fit."

Mary pushed through the front door wiping her hands on a flour sack apron. Her pretty face broke into a smile.

"Afternoon, Ma'am."

"Good afternoon, George. Would you drink a cup of coffee?"

"That would shore sit mighty fine, Ma'am."

Mary disappeared into the house while T. J. nodded toward a rough-hewn chair on the porch.

"It's been more'n a week. I'm guessing you didn't find him."

"Nope. We rode in late last night. We tracked him all the way to the Canadian River up where the Indian Territory starts. It galled me something awful to have to turn around but I was way out of my jurisdiction. This County Sheriff's badge don't mean squat up there."

"How's old Isaac?"

"Doc says he'll recover. They buried Deputy Mason while we were gone. I shouldn't have left him by himself. In hindsight, I should'da had two guards on that fellow."

"It wasn't your fault, George."

"You're still going after them ain't you?"

"Sure as God made green apples."

"When you got in mind to leave?"

"Come morning"

Mary pushed through the door carrying a tray with two slabs of pie and coffee. "I thought you men might like a piece of fresh pumpkin pie."

"Sure sounds fine, ma'am. It's worth the twenty mile ride just for a piece of your pie."

"I doubt if they're quite that good."

"Any idea where that Dutton fellow was headed?" T. J. asked.

"Yeah, I didn't get a chance to tell you. He spilt his guts the night before he escaped. Told me Bob would likely head for their home place over in the Indian Territory. It's on the North Canadian River about a day's ride northeast of a place called Antelope Hills on the South Canadian. He said his brother was sweet on a bargirl named May Belle over in Enid at a saloon called the Lucky Lady."

"I'm obliged," T. J. told his friend. "That ought to help."

Mary stood silently and listened, then dropped her head to hide sad tears and retreated quickly into the house.

Long after the sheriff's dust had settled in the distance T. J. continued to set in silence staring off into nothingness. He knew inside the house Mary would be lying across the bed, her face smothered in a tear soaked pillow. He wanted to rush to her, to gather her in his arms, to kiss away the tears, to try to explain why he had to go away again, one more time. Instead, he swallowed the last sip of the cold coffee and continued to stare off into the distance.

"Pa...Pa."

Tad's concerned voice invaded T. J.'s scrambled thoughts. "Pa, are you okay?"

He blinked his mind back to focus and saw both Tad and Lupe staring at him with concern occupying their faces.

"You reckon me and Lupe could go down to the creek and fish for awhile? We've got an awful lot of wood split and stacked and we can help the girls dig them turnips for Ma after we get back. Do you think we might could?"

"I reckon that would be all right, it's a warm afternoon."

"Thanks, Pa. Want to come with us?"

"Reckon not this time."

He watched absently as the boys gathered their fishing poles and slung them over their shoulders and headed for the creek. He knew he could wait no longer. He pushed wearily from his rocker and headed into the house.

She was there just like he knew she would be, lying stomach down across the bed, her face buried in her pillow. He sat down beside her and gently placed a hand on her shoulder.

"I'm sorry you had to hear it like that," he whispered hoarsely.

For a long minute she didn't reply, then between sobs, she turned her tear stained face toward him. "When...when were you going to tell me?" She pleaded.

"Mary, I just ain't got the words to explain why I got to do what I got to do. Ain't nothing in the world I'd rather do than to spend what time I got left right here with you and the kids, don't you know that?

"These past few days have been some of the best days in my whole life. Maybe it's the knowing how little time we've got left that makes it more special, I don't know, but I never knowed a man could be so happy, that life could be so good.

"But I know how hard times will get after I'm gone. Lupe being here ought to help some but not enough. I just can't stand the thought of leaving you with no way to take care of you and the family. I promise you, this will be my last trip. Soon as I get back we'll sit on the front porch and watch the kids grow."

Gently he lifted her up and gathered her in his arms. She melted against him, burying her face in the softness of his shoulder. For a long time he held her, caressing, comforting, consoling.

CHAPTER XVII

By the time the ashen grayness of false dawn lightened the sky T. J. had said his good-byes and was several miles closer toward the eastern horizon. It had been hard. Hugs, tears, and parting looks tore his heart out by the roots. He hated leaving the family, but he had to do what he had to do.

The big buckskin tossed its huge head and tugged at the reins, begging to run. Old Solomon plodded along behind seemingly unconcerned with the heavy packsaddle he carried.

The hard-fought dawn struggled up from dark shadows of the distant hills. The day it gave birth to was a sorry excuse. It was neither light nor dark, only a sickly slate gray, which matched T. J.'s mood perfectly.

Endless miles and miles of east Texas prairie occupied the day, and the next, and the next one after that. By noon of the third day he reined up on the banks of the South Canadian River. He hadn't seen a living soul the whole trip. A line of stunted, low-lying knolls off to his right figured to be the Antelope Hills George had mentioned. He headed that direction.

He made camp at sundown beside a little running stream in a grove of young sycamore. After tending to his horses, he put on a pot of coffee and sliced some salt pork and turnips into a pan. After supper he settled against his saddle with a cup of coffee and thought about home.

Reckon supper is over by now. Mary and the girls would be doing the dishes. The boys are likely doing their schooling. Won't be long till bedtime. Shore would be good to stretch out beside Mary. He propped another stick of wood on the fire and pulled the blanket up and closed his eyes.

Bob Dutton couldn't stand it any longer. He had patched up the corral good enough to hold his newly acquired horses, got the rusty pump working, and piled most of the trash into the second room of the old home place. But he had long since emptied the last of his whiskey supply and he was a man that got thirsty real often. Besides, he had a strong hankering to see May Belle. Settling it in his mind he saddled the bay mare and climbed into the saddle. It was a forty mile ride to Enid but by pushing the mare hard he covered the distance in half the usual time.

It was mid-afternoon when Bob swung from his saddle and tied the bay in front of the Lucky Lady Saloon. On the boardwalk he paused to roll a smoke. Putting fire to it he allowed a slow, cautious gaze to crawl along the busy street. Nothing seemed out of order.

Enid was a typical trail town whose only excuse for existence was that it was situated close to the Chisholm Trail used by Texas cattlemen to drive their herds to Kansas. Two lines of unpainted, flatboard buildings stared at each other across a single dusty street. The drovers used the small town as a resupply stop and a place to blow off steam after long weeks on the trail. As such, it had a reputation as one of those tough trail towns.

The U. S. Marshals out of Judge Isaac Parker's court in Fort Smith enforced the law in the whole Indian Territory, but they were spread so thin Enid had hired its own law dog. He was a tough old codger that generally left a fellow alone unless somebody killed somebody.

May Belle was sipping a drink with a young looking cowboy at a back table. She glanced up as he headed toward the bar. A wide smile of recognition puckered her red lips.

"Whiskey. Bring the bottle," he told the barrel-shaped barkeep.

"It's been awhile since we seen you in town," the barman said, setting the bottle in front of Bob and making change for the double-eagle.

"Yeah, I reckon."

"Been traveling?"

"Yeah, some. Who's the jasper with May Belle?"

"He's been around a month or so. Name's Catlin from Abilene. Most likely dropped off of one of the trail crews."

"Him and May Belle been spending a lot of time together?"

"She gets paid to spend time with the customers."

"Get her over here."

"She's busy."

"I said, *get her over here.*" The last words were forced through clenched teeth accompanied by a look that made the bartender turn pale.

"May belle," he called and motioned for her.

Bob watched her linger for a long moment and whisper something to the young cowboy before pushing from the chair and sauntering over to the bar. She was something. She had long, bright red hair and a beautiful face. Her waist was so tiny Bob could encircle it with both hands. She walked with a flirty swagger that swished her hips from side-to-side and had a way about her that made every customer believe he was the most special man that ever walked.

"Can't you see I'm busy, Fred?"

A single nod of the barkeep's head in Bob's direction caused her gaze to follow. She headed that way but looked none to happy about it.

"You too busy for me all of a sudden?" Bob asked angrily.

"Of course not, I saw you come in but I was busy."

"So I see."

"You've been gone over two months. You walk in and I'm supposed to just drop everything and run into your arms?"

"I've got a bottle. Let's go upstairs."

May Belle hesitated. Her emerald-green gaze flicked to the cowboy at the table, then to the barkeep.

"Sure," she finally said, breaking an obviously forced smile across her pretty face. "I'll just go tell Fred."

"I'll tell Fred," Bob told her firmly, taking hold of her arm roughly with one hand and scooping up his bottle with the other.

"We'll be upstairs awhile," he said over a shoulder as he guided May Belle roughly toward the stairs. "See to it somebody gets that red bay down to the livery for me."

"Hey! You there!" the cowboy shouted and pushed to his feet, knocking over his chair. "She's with me,"

Bob Dutton stopped and hesitated for a long moment. His first instinct was to just shoot the cowboy and get it over and done with. But then he'd have to deal with the Marshal and that would mess up his time with May Belle. Instead, he shoved May Belle up the stairs and called over his shoulder.

"Maybe she was. But now she's with me and we'll be awhile."

Amos Dutton sat impatiently on the stolen pinto in a willow thicket beside the river and stared silently at the darkened house. He had watched their old home place for more than half an hour and had seen no movement. If his brother was inside he was asleep or most likely drunk.

Two horses milled about in the corral. *Reckon where he come by them?*

Glancing up at the white moon he judged it to be near midnight. *Should I bed down out here till morning and see if he's around or try to slip up on him and take a chance of getting my head blowed off?*

He still hadn't made up his mind what to do about his brother. It was still hard to believe his own kin had took his horse and left him to die or get captured, but then, with Bob, you could never tell what he would do. *Sometimes I think Bob is half crazy.*

After watching for another few minutes he decided it best to bed down in the willow thicket and see how things looked in the morning. Loosening the cinch straps and sliding the saddle onto the ground, he rolled up in his saddle blanket and was asleep in minutes.

Amos roused himself awake just short of good daylight. He jerked upright and pinned the little cabin with a searching gaze. There still was no sign of life. Drawing his stolen pistol, he left the pinto where it was tied and crept cautiously toward the cabin.

It was clear somebody, most likely his brother, had patched up the corral that held the two horses. *Maybe somebody else has moved in,* he considered. *Better not be.*

At the front porch he paused and listened for a long moment before easing up the two steps onto the porch. *Still no sign of anybody around.* Holding his pistol out in front of him he gently lifted the latch and pushed open the door with the toe of his boot. *Somebody has been here, but looks like they're gone now. If it was Bob, where would he be?*

* * *

Before the sky paled T. J. had breakfast over and was in the saddle. He rode steady, keeping the buckskin's nose pointed northwest. The country around him had changed drastically. Gone were the flat plains of east Texas, replaced by thick stands of blackjack, willow, and sycamore. Heavy brush clogged the trail and made progress slow.

He found the rundown cabin on the bank of the North Canadian River just before sundown. The structure wasn't much. Except for two hungry looking horses in the corral, the place appeared deserted.

T. J. stepped from the saddle and squatted on the ground for a closer look. He fingered the tracks. *Not very old, a day, maybe two.* The signs showed someone had lived here recently, maybe for as long as three or four weeks, but had left three or four days ago. A second person—he figured Amos Dutton—had arrived two days earlier and had left just a day or two ahead of T. J. He decided to rest the night and head out on their trail come first light.

It was good dark when Amos reined up at the livery in Enid and stabled the pinto. He paid the grouchy old liveryman and fingered the last dollar he had to his name. Figuring if his brother was in town he would be at the Lucky Lady saloon, he limped that way.

A half-dozen bar girls worked the crowd in the saloon but Amos didn't see May Belle among them. Elbowing his way across the room he shouldered up to the bar.

"Whiskey," he told the barkeep, pushing his last dollar across the polished surface. "You seen my brother, Bob Dutton, around lately?"

The bar-dog glanced up. "Yeah, I seen him. He's been laid up with my best girl for three days. Only time they been out of that room was to eat now and then and get a couple more bottles."

Amos's gaze followed the barman's nod up the stairs.

"Reckon I might better check on 'em, just to make shore they be still alive and kickin'."

"Better duck if you do. He throwed a whiskey bottle at me when I went up to check on them yesterday. They've both tied on a humdinger."

Amos found the room by the broken bottle in the hallway. He loosed the pistol in his holster just in case, and rapped on the door.

"Go away," a slurred response from inside reached his hearing.

"Bob, this is Amos. Open the door."

A long space of silence almost convinced Amos he hadn't heard.

"Amos, is that really you?"

"Yeah, it's me. *Open the door!*"

It took several minutes before the key turned in the lock and the door swung open a crack.

Amos pushed the door open angrily and stomped into the room. The first thing he saw was the pistol in his brother's fist. The next thing he saw was May Belle trying to hide her nakedness with a bed sheet and not doing a very good job of it. His gaze fixed on the sight.

"Amos? I thought you was . . .

"Dead? Yeah, I know. I 'bout was. Why'd you do that to me, Bob?"

"Do what?"

"Why'd you run off with my horse and leave me there to die or get caught by the law?"

"Who told you that?"

"That Sheriff! That's who! They said you took my horse and left me so you could outrun them by switching horses."

"And you believed them?"

"I didn't know what to believe. All I know is I would have hung if I hadn't busted out of that jail down in Lubbock."

"Well they lied to you little brother. I left you hid and took your horse to lead them away from you. When I come back you was gone. I didn't know what happened to you. I wouldn't run out on my own kin."

"I didn't think so but, I didn't know what to think."

"Here, little brother, have a drink. You remember, May Belle don't you?"

"Yeah, uh, I remember."

"Come join us. We'll all have a drink and celebrate."

Feeling sorry for the two horses in the corral, T. J. watered them good and hobbled them on some nearby grass before riding out early the following morning. *A man that won't care for his horses ain't much of a man*, he thought as he rode away.

All day he followed their trail. Both riders headed the same direction. Northeast. Just after sundown he rode down the single street of Enid, Oklahoma Territory. A light drizzle was starting to fall and a cold wind sent shivers over him. *Looks like it's gonna be a cold, miserable night.*

Enid looked like any of a hundred trail towns: A single hotel, maybe a dozen assorted businesses, and half that many saloons. The livery stable was easy enough to find and he stepped down just outside the double doors.

"Hello inside," he called out.

"Keep your shirt on," a grumpy voice from inside replied. "I'm a comin'"

The liveryman was old, small and lopsided. He hobbled along with a limp and one shoulder hung slumped. *Most likely crippled up by a horse as contrary as he sounds,* T. J. thought.

"I need my horse and pack mule grain fed and stalled for the night."

"That'll be two dollars, in advance."

Stripping his saddlebags, rifle, and the sawed-off double barrel shotgun from the saddle, T. J. dug the two dollars out of his pocket and handed it to the old liveryman. As he turned he spotted Lupe's pinto in the corral.

"Fine looking pinto there in the corral."

The old fellow cut a quick glance that direction. "Yeah. Don't belong to me though."

"Kind of looking for a horse something like that for my boy. Reckon the owner might be interested in selling?"

"Wouldn't know. Big fellow, name's Dutton. Looked like he headed for the Lucky Lady."

"I'm obliged. Might just look him up."

The Enid Hotel was a two-story, boxy structure of weathered lumber. T. J. pushed through the front door and was greeted by the desk clerk. He was a gangling man with bony features with a look of annoyance at being interrupted from a nap.

"I need a room."

"Two dollars a day in advance. Room six upstairs."

"That sounds a mite steep for a two-bit room."

"Take it or leave it. Makes no difference to me."

T. J. dug two dollars from his pocket and pitched them on the counter and signed the registration book. Scooping up his key T. J. climbed the stairs and found his room. A rusty iron bedstead, a washstand with a pan and pitcher, and a single straight-back chair, that's all his two dollars bought him. Checking the sheets on the bed, he was surprised to find they were actually clean.

After a week on the trail eating his own cooking, he decided it was time for a change. Leaving his saddlebags, rifle, and the scattergun, he locked the door and went in search of supper.

The Cattlemen's Café was small, clean, and crowded. The heavyset waitress greeted him with a wide grin and a cup of steaming coffee.

"What will it be for you, stranger?"

"Do I have a choice?"

"Of course, she chuckled. The choice is beef steak, fried potatoes, and turnip greens or do without."

"Then I reckon I'll take beef steak, fried potatoes, and turnip greens."

"Good choice. None of my business, but are you okay? You don't look so good."

"Well, I'm better than I look, but thanks for the concern."

"Maybe my supper will perk you up."

"Bet it will at that."

The coffee scalded his lips and burned all the way down but warmed his innards as it soaked in. While he blowed the steam away he looked the crowd over. They looked like local folks and cowboys. Amos Dutton was not among them.

The food was better than good. He took his time and ate slowly. When he finished he paid for his supper and left a generous tip.

"Keep the coffee hot," he told the friendly waitress. "I'll be back."

He was bone tired and chilled through and through. *I shore could use a good night's sleep,"* he thought as he pushed open the door of the little Café.. *I'll wait until tomorrow to start looking for the Dutton brothers.*

Lamplight from inside spilled onto the boardwalk and framed a giant presence about to enter the Café. It was Amos Dutton.

Having only seen T. J. once—and that when he was only half conscious—it took a minute before recognition widened the big man's eyes. By that time T. J.'s Colt was jammed deep into his ribs.

"Well, well. Lookie what we have here."

"Who are you?"

"I'm the last man this side of Hell you wanted to run into."

"Don't know what you're talking about."

"Let's step into that alley and I'll explain it so even you can understand it."

Shoving the killer in front of him, T. J. forced him into the alley beside the Cafe and relieved him of his pistol.

"I've got a wanted poster in my pocket that says you're worth five hundred dollars dead or alive."

"You a bounty hunter?"

"Yep. Got a flier on your brother too. Where is he?"

"Ain't telling you nothin'"

Shoving the giant roughly against the wall T. J. jammed the Colt under Amos's chin and thumbed back the hammer, forcing his head up, stretching his neck, and whispered in a raspy voice.

"Now you listen to me and you listen real close. I'd just as soon kill you right here, right now, and save the hassle of hauling you all the way back to Texas. You can make the trip in the saddle or across it, makes no difference to me. Now I'm gonna ask you just one more time. Where's that no good brother of yours?"

"Go to Hell."

The Colt in T. J.'s fist lashed out striking the big man across the face. The unmistakable snap of bone cartilage made a sickly sound as the lick shattered Amos's nose. Again the pistol arched through the darkness and landed a crushing blow. Blood and tooth fragments splattered the side of the building. Again and again T. J. swung until the killer lay in a crumpled heap in the mud.

"That's for what you done to the old liveryman in Lubbock. He's a friend of mine."

"No more," Amos begged through busted lips. "He's with his girl upstairs at the Lucky Lady."

"Get up!"

The man climbed unsteadily to his feet, spitting blood, his eyes glinting with a poisonous stare.

"Let's go," T. J. told him, prodding him along with the nose of his pistol toward the Town Marshal's office and shoved him through the door.

The Marshal was a man whose looks told a fellow he had been up and down the trail a few times.

He was wide-shouldered and thick through the chest. His salt and pepper hair and handlebar mustache framed a leathered face with turkey tracks framing both eyes. Right now those eyes were pinned on T. J. with a questioning look.

"What's this all about?" The Marshal asked.

"This is Amos Dutton," T. J. said, withdrawing the wanted flier on the two brothers and pitching it onto the Marshal's desk. "Him and his brother are wanted in Lubbock, Texas for murdering a doctor and his wife. They also killed a deputy sheriff and pistol whipped a helpless old liveryman and stole my boy's pinto. I found it down at the livery. I'm taking them both back to hang. I need you to hold on to this one for me until I gather up his brother."

"And who might you be?"

"Name's Littlejohn, T. J. Littlejohn."

"You a bounty man, Mr. Littlejohn?"

"I've been called lots of things. Something wrong with that?"

"Never had much use for them myself. How'd he get all beat up like that?"

"He put up a fight."

"Appears to me the fight was kind of one-sided. You say the other brother is here in town too?"

"Yep."

"Need some help?"

"Nope."

The lawman's mustache lifted at one corner in something close to a smile. "Kinda thought not. Just make sure you don't cross the line, do we understand one another?"

"That poster says *dead or alive*. I reckon it's their choice.

* * *

With Amos locked safely in the Marshal's jail, T. J. headed for the hotel. The earlier drizzle had turned to a steady cold rain. *Reckon I might just as well get this over and done with,* he thought as he climbed the stairs to his room. Inside, he snatched up the sawed-off scattergun, thumbed two shells in and snapped it closed with a flip of his wrist. He stuffed a handful of extra shotgun shells in his pocket and headed back downstairs.

Up the street he stopped just outside the batwing doors of the Lucky Lady Saloon and peered inside. He swept the room with a look The place was crowded. Men anxious to lose their hard earned money waited two deep at the gaming tables. A half-dozen painted up bar girls with hollow eyes and haggard looks worked the room.

He had never seen Bob Dutton and wouldn't know the man if he saw him, but he knew the type. Several in the room fit that description. *How am I gonna find him? Reckon the best thing to do is just ask.*

Thirsty cowboys stood shoulder-to-shoulder along the long bar. Two busy bartenders were having trouble keeping up with the business. T. J. shouldered his way to the bar and squeezed into an empty spot.

"What'll it be?" The graying barkeep asked, wiping the bar.

"A beer and some information," T. J. said hoarsely, plopping the sawed-off scattergun on the bar in front of him. Faces at the bar turned and took one look at the speaker and the shotgun then quietly made some space.

"The information's free, the beer ain't. You pay in advance here." the barkeep said as he set the beer on the bar.

"Seems the way everybody does business in this town. Know a fellow by the name of Bob Dutton?" T. J. asked, dropping two bits on the bar and watching the barkeeper's reaction closely.

Instinctively, the man's eyes flicked upstairs then looked quickly away before replying.

"Nope, never heard of him."

"What about a bar girl named May Belle? Don't suppose you know her either?"

"Yeah, but she's...busy."

"Is her room upstairs?"

"Yeah, but you can't go up there. I done told you she's busy."

Without touching the beer T. J. scooped up the shotgun and headed for the stairs. The big barman shouted at his back and hurried to stop him. Just as T. J. reached the foot of the stairs the big man grabbed his shoulder roughly. In the space of an eye blink T. J. wheeled and jammed the nose of the shotgun under the barkeep's fat chin and thumbed back both hammers.

"You best tend to your own business, Mister."

The man's face drained of all color, leaving it the shade of white biscuit dough. His open hands slowly raised as he backed away. Keeping one eye on the hushed crowd, T.J. slowly climbed the stairs.

Four doors opened into a short hallway. A fifth opened to steps leading down to the alley. Creeping along the hallway and pausing in front of each door, the rhythmic squeak of a bed told him which room was occupied.

A thin grin curled T. J.'s lips. *Good a time as any I reckon,* he thought as he lifted a booted foot and kicked in the door.

The man in the bed had nothing on except his red longjohns. The pretty redheaded girl was naked as the day she was born. Both snapped their heads around to stare wide-eyed as the door slammed inward.

"Don't move!" T. J. ordered. "I'm looking for Bob Dutton."

"Who're you?" the man snarled.

"Get up and get your clothes on."

Instead, Dutton rolled off the bed pulling the girl with him.

At the same time he grabbed a holstered pistol from a bedside table. Using the screaming girl as a shield, the killer snapped off a quick shot that missed by mere inches. T. J. couldn't return fire for fear of hitting the girl. His only choice was to duck back through the shattered doorway. Two more shots tore through the paper-thin wall of the hallway.

"Give it up, Dutton. You got nowhere to go."

Shattering glass told T. J. he had been wrong about that. The killer had jumped through the second story window. Snapping a quick look around the doorframe, he saw the girl cowing naked on the floor. Racing to the window T. J. looked down into the street in time to see the outlaw limping badly and grabbing the reins of a horse from the hitching rail in front of the saloon.

If he fired the scattergun it would kill or injure several of the other horses. Shifting the shotgun into his left hand he snatched the Colt from its holster and snapped off two shots that were both off their mark as the killer galloped away.

Wheeling, T. J. ran back through the door and down the hallway to the outside steps. Taking them two at a time he burst from the alley into the street. Without paying any mind to the spectators that had poured out of the saloon, T. J. hurried to the hotel to collect his rifle and saddlebags. The Marshal was waiting in the street for him when he came back down carrying his gear.

"I'm taking it he got away?"

"Ain't hardly likely," T. J. told him as he hurried past the lawman toward the livery. "You just hang onto the other one till I get back."

In a few short minutes he had the buckskin saddled and cinched. He decided to leave the mule and pick it up later. Sleeving into his rain slicker he toed a stirrup and heeled his horse into a short lope east out of town. One thing for sure, barefooted, with no hat and wearing nothing but his longjohns Bob Dutton wouldn't get far on a night like this.

Even in the pale light of an occasional half moon, the tracks in the muddy road were easy to follow. T. J. pulled the collar of his rain slicker tighter around his neck and kept his gaze glued to the ground. He had gone no more than three miles when the tracks veered toward a farmhouse that set off the road a quarter mile or so. The shadowy outline of a large barn with a hayloft stood out against a heavy night sky. The muddy tracks led that direction. It was obvious Dutton had sought shelter in the barn from the brutal weather.

Reining up, T. J. dismounted and looped the reins around the split rail of a corral that adjoined the barn. The big double doors of the barn were closed but the tracks led inside.

Thumbing back both hammers of the shotgun he flattened his back against the wall of the barn and cracked open one of the doors. Fully expecting the action to bring shots he was surprised when no sound came from inside.

Creeping to the partially open door he braced himself, darted around the edge of the opening and dove headlong into the pitch blackness. A fiery-red bloom blossomed from the hayloft above him. A rifle bullet tore into the barn door just above his head. Twisting his body T. J. rolled to his left and lay completely still.

An ominous hush permeated the darkness. The air was thick and still. The only sound was the steady drumming of rain on the metal roof and the nervous movement of a horse somewhere nearby. The musty smell of hay and horse manure that he was lying in stung his nose but he dare not move. He waited. Minutes seemed like hours.

The soft creak of a board told him the killer was moving. T. J.'s muscles tightened. He swallowed the lump in his throat and tightened his finger on the trigger of the double-barreled shotgun and waited. When he heard the gentle touch of bare feet on a board he knew Dutton was climbing slowly down the ladder. Straining his hearing he tried to pinpoint the exact location of the sound.

A slight scraping sound gave him his answer and he triggered off one barrel of the double-barreled shotgun. At the same instant he flung his body further to his left in a roll. The blast from the shotgun lit up the interior of the barn in a reddish glow long enough to see his shot had missed. A rifle bullet smacked into the spot he had just vacated with a soft thud. Before the light faded he saw Dutton dive into a nearby horse stall.

It suddenly dawned on T. J. how quick on the trigger the man was. *Maybe I can use that fast reaction to my advantage. You don't suppose he would fall for the oldest trick in the book?*

"What's going on in there?" a loud voice from outside the barn shouted.

Using the distraction, T. J. swiped off his hat and sailed it off to his right. Immediately Dutton's rifle barked and spewed red-hot flame and lead at the sound. In the space of a heartbeat T. J. squeezed the trigger of the Stevens shotgun. The heavy double-aught pellets splintered the boards of the stall and slammed the outlaw in a staggering backward dance into the other side of the stall. A pitiful scream shattered the darkness and faded into a low gurgled moan.

Pushing quickly to his feet T. J., ejected the spent shotgun shells and thumbed in two fresh loads while easing cautiously toward the moaning sound. One long, gasping breath reached his hearing, then there was nothing but silence. Bob Dutton had drawn his last breath.

CHAPTER XVIII

The nights were long and slow to die. At least during the day Mary could stay busy and give her mind brief moments of rest from worrying about everything. Not true of the nights. She spent most of every night tossing and turning, worrying, and weeping.

She worried about T. J.: *Where is he? Is he safe? Has he had another spell? Is he someplace warm and dry tonight? How much longer will he be with us?* She worried about her and the children: *What will we do without T. J.? How will we survive? How can I raise the children without him? Will we lose the farm? Where will we live?*

She lay in the darkness of her bedroom, staring intently at nothing. Her husband's name worked its way up her throat on a sob. "Oh T. J."

Tears scorched hot trails down her cheeks. She balled the quilt in her fists and wept silently and open-mouthed, shaking with spasms of hopelessness, smothering the sobs to keep the children from hearing.

At some point she fell into an exhausted sleep only to drift into a troubled dream, turning her sleep into a place of fear, stealing away whatever peace the night could offer.

She dreamed of a world without her husband, felt the excruciating pain of his death, experienced the heart wrenching sorrow of walking away from his grave, felt the confusion of days without his wisdom and guidance, and of the dreaded nights of loneliness.

Consciousness came slowly with the first light of dawn. She blinked herself awake and thanked the Lord it was only a dream, but one that would surely soon become a reality. Her nightgown was wet with perspiration.

Pushing herself wearily from the bed, exhausted from the restless night, she stripped off the dampened gown and dressed for the day. Lighting the coal oil lamp she tiptoed to the kitchen and hurriedly built a fire in the old cook stove. A fleeting picture of the new stove she had dreamed of for so long flashed through her mind but was immediately pushed aside. *No use thinking about that now,* she thought.

The coffee was boiling by the time Marilyn walked in all sleepy-eyed.

"Would you wake the boys for me?" Mary asked.

"Oh ma, they always gripe me out."

"Tell them I said it's almost daylight. It's time to get up."

"Okay, but if they throw a pillow at me I'm going to throw it back."

In only moments happy screams of laughter came from the boy's room. Marilyn raced through the kitchen with both boys in their red longjohns right on her heels, pounding her backside with the pillows in their hands. A smile broke across Mary's face. The distraction from her troubling thoughts felt good.

* * *

The morning sun was two hours old when T. J. rode into Enid. The rain had moved out sometime during the night and the morning broke bright and clear. After explaining everything to the farmer the man had allowed T. J. to spend the rest of the night in the hayloft. It was a welcome relief, he was dog tired.

He had had another vomiting spell during the night. The spell hadn't been as bad as before, but it left him drained of energy.

A crowd of curious townspeople poured out of the shops and saloons as he rode down the street leading the horse Dutton had stolen. Draped belly down across the saddle lay Dutton's body, at least what was left of it.

It was a gruesome sight. The heavy shotgun pellets had torn away a good part of the top half of the killer's body. What was left was a mass of torn flesh that had bled itself dry and turned a sickly purple. Women gasped and turned away.

Reining up in front of the Marshal's office T. J. climbed stiffly from the saddle and looped the reins of both horses around the hitching rail. A crowd of gawkers quickly gathered.

"I'm guessing that's Dutton?" the Marshal asked as he emerged from his office.

"Yep."

Striding over to the body the lawman fisted a handful of blood caked hair and lifted the head. His eyebrows skewed together and a half-dozen lines plowed furrows across his forehead. It looked like he was about to lose his breakfast.

"Good Lord, Man! What'd you shoot him with? There ain't enough left to bother to bury."

"To my way of thinking he don't deserve burying but do what you want with him, he's yours now. I'll need a signed affidavit saying I turned him over to you so I can collect the reward."

"Burt, how about taking him over to the undertaker for me? Come on into the office, Mr. Littlejohn and I'll see to that affidavit."

T. J. followed the marshal into his office and took a seat. The marshal took out a legal looking paper and started writing.

"That horse he's on is the one he stole last night," T. J. said.

"That reminds me, he rode into town on a red bay mare. It's down at the livery. I reckon it's yours if you want to claim it."

"The pinto Amos stole from my boy is there too. I'll be taking it back with me."

"When you figure on heading back?"

"I need to rest up tonight. I'll be taking my prisoner and leaving at first light."

"I'll have him ready."

With the affidavit in his pocket T. J. stopped off at the telegraph office and sent a wire to George Paxton in Lubbock, then headed for the Cattlemen's Café.

The friendly waitress's face broke a grin as he pushed through the door and took his choice of tables that were all empty. She brought a pot of coffee and a cup and poured it full.

"Do you always cause this much excitement when you ride into town?"

"It's been a busy couple of days," he told her, blowing at his coffee. "I shore could use a good breakfast."

"Just you relax and enjoy your coffee. I'll fix you right up."

"Where you from?" she asked over her shoulder as she headed for the kitchen.

"Lubbock," he told her as loudly as his raspy voice would allow. "That's down in Texas."

"They say you're a bounty hunter. You don't look like one. I had you pegged for a family man with something bad ailing him."

"Yeah, you're right on both counts."

He was finishing up his second cup when the waitress set a heaping plateful of ham, eggs, and hot biscuits in front of him.

"If that don't fix you up nothing will," she said.

"I'm obliged," he told her, forking a generous slice of ham to his mouth.

True to his word the marshal had Amos hand shackled and ready to ride when T. J. led his three horses and pack mule up to the office just after daybreak.

"It's a mighty long way to Texas," the lawman told him, handing him the key to the shackles. "Reckon you can get him back okay?"

"I'll get him back, one way or the other."

"Yeah, I reckon you will at that," the marshal said, nodding his head. "You ride easy. You hear? And try not to visit my town again. We ain't use to this much excitement around here."

T. J. shook a single nod and helped Amos into the saddle of the bay. He booted a stirrup and gathered up the reins to the bay and lead rope to the pinto. The street was empty as they headed quietly out of town.

Not a single word passed between him and the killer until they reined up at the deserted Dutton place late that afternoon. The two horses he had hobbled were still grazing nearby. He helped Amos out of the saddle and allowed him to relieve himself while he saddled the two extra horses and tied them on lead ropes.

He helped his prisoner into the saddle and tied both ankles to the stirrups. Taking a lariat rope from one of the saddles he looped it around Dutton's neck and wrapped the loose end around his own saddle horn. Pulling the wanted poster from his shirt pocket he held it up in front of the giant.

"Just so you understand. This flier says you're worth the same to me *dead or alive*. Makes no difference to me. If I even get the notion you're thinking about escaping I'll shoot you right between the eyes. You got it?"

The big man didn't say a word, just stared with hatred boiling out of his eyes. T. J. climbed into the saddle and they headed for Texas.

"We're gonna ride a ways tonight."

Mary and Marilyn had just finished the weekly wash and were hanging the wet clothes on the line. Tad and Lupe were bringing in the last of the turnip crop and spreading them in the barn. As usual, Sally was swinging in her swing.

"Mama. Somebody's coming," Sally shouted and pointed toward the creek.

Tad and Lupe heard her and snatched up they're rifles and came running. They all stared off into the distance, straining to make out the single rider approaching the creek on the far side.

"It's the Sheriff," Tad announced.

Mary's heart leaped into her throat, fearing the worst. Dread coiled inside her stomach, twisting and squirming like a snake. Chills rippled down her back. She hardly breathed until George rode into the yard and greeted them cheerfully, touching a thumb and curled finger to the brim of his hat.

"Afternoon, Mary. Looks like you ladies have had a rough day."

"Good day to you, George. If you had got here a little sooner we would have let you help with the washing," Mary told him smiling.

"Yeah," the sheriff chuckled. "I've been waiting over yonder on the hill for the last two hours until you got finished."

"Oh you have not," Mary laughed. "Get down and set a spell.

Marilyn, warm up the coffee, would you? What brings you out this way?"

"Got a telegram from T. J. Thought you'd be anxious to read it," he told her, climbing down and handing her the folded paper.

Unfolding it she read it anxiously. "It says he will be in Lubbock on Saturday. He wants us to meet him in town with the wagon. Wonder what that's all about?"

"Don't know. I wondered that too. He got both of the Dutton brothers. He's bringing the big one back to stand trial."

"Yes, I saw that. I'm so relieved."

"I knew you'd be happy to hear that he's okay."

"Yes. We're just finishing up here. Would you stay for supper?"

"Well, to be honest with you ma'am, I was kinda hoping you would ask."

After two helpings of beans, turnips and fried potatoes, George pushed back from the table. "Mighty fine meal, Ma'am. Don't know when I've ate better."

"That's what you say every time you eat with us, George."

"Yes, ma'am, and it's still the gospel truth."

"Well, let's take our coffee out to the porch. Marilyn and the boys will clean the table."

The night air was a little nippy and Mary slipped a shawl around her shoulders and fluffed her long blonde hair out from under the shawl with a stroke of her hand. She showed the sheriff to T. J.'s rocking chair and settled in the straight-back chair nearby.

"You folks shore got a pretty place out here."

"I fell in love with the valley the first time T. J. and I rode over the hill and saw it. I don't know what we'll do when he's . . ." Her words trailed off, leaving the rest unsaid.

"Mary, I'm...I'm shore sorry about T. J., we've been friends a long time."

"I know. He's told me many times what a good friend you are."

"Did you notice in the telegram that he got the boy's pinto back?"

"Yes. Lupe was so excited. He really loves that horse."

"How's he working out?"

"He's like one of the family. I don't know how we ever got along without him. He's such a hard worker and him and Tad are like brothers."

"That's fine. He sure seems like a good boy. Glad he's working out."

"It's none of my business, but how are you and Justine Reynolds getting along? She's been a widow almost two years now hasn't she?"

"Something like that I reckon. Aw, she's a nice enough lady I suppose. But to be honest with you, she's just not my type."

"Oh really? I'm sorry to hear that. I was kind of hoping you two would hit it off."

"Naw, she's a little pushy for my liking. I'm kind of set in my ways I reckon. Would it bother you if I smoke, Ma'am?"

"Not at all. But I surely would appreciate it if you'd stop calling me *Ma'am*. As long as we've known each other I'd like to think we would have progressed to, *Mary*."

"Then Mary it will be from now on."

"You said Justine wasn't your type. I can't help being curious, George, what would you look for in a wife?"

"Hard question. Please don't take this wrong, Mary, but I reckon I'd have to say she would have to be someone like you."

George rolled a smoke and lit it, drawing a deep inhale. For a long space of time they sat through a comfortable silence, staring off into the night and listening to the whip-o-wills. Inside, they heard the children's happy laughter.

"That shore sounds good," the lawman said.

"The children? Yes, they keep things lively."

"I always wanted kids."

"They're a joy to have around. They keep one's mind off things."

"Well, I best be heading on back to town, I reckon."

"No sense in you riding back tonight, why don't you bed down in the hayloft and wait until morning?"

"No I...I appreciate the offer, Mary, but I reckon I better ride on back," he said as he pushed from the chair. "I got some things I need to do first thing in the morning. I 'm shore obliged for the supper though. I reckon we'll see you folks on Saturday."

"We'll be there. I'm so grateful to you for bringing the telegram."

"You're shore welcome. Say my good-bye's to the kids for me."

Mary watched the sheriff until he was swallowed up by the darkness then turned and went inside.

CHAPTER XIX

Saturday finally came. Well before good light Mary and the kids were up and headed toward town. Even so, she figured it would be mid-morning before they would arrive. Excitement and anticipation grew with each turn of the wagon wheel.

Word had spread about T. J.'s expected arrival and that he was bringing back the hated killer for trial. It seemed everyone within a fifty mile radius was in town when Mary and the kids pulled down the street. The stores and saloons were crowded. It was almost like a carnival atmosphere.

After the boys unhitched the mules and turned them into the livery corral they and the girls all ran off someplace with their friends. Mary strolled over to the General Store to look around. Wiley and Doris Stubblefield seemed especially excited to see her almost bubbly. She was still browsing among the dress material when someone outside shouted, "Here they come!"

Others took up the cry. People poured from the stores and saloons and crowded into the narrow street, jostling to get a better view. Young people scampered onto rooftops. Mary tiptoed to see over the crowd. Off in the distance she caught a glimpse of the little wad of horses with T. J. in the lead.

To say she was proud would have been a vast understatement. She was filled with emotions: Relief, gratitude, and thankfulness to the Almighty surged through her.

As T. J. and his little procession breached the edge of town and people saw the killer close up, his hands shackled and with a rope around his neck they began to react in anger. The crowd turned ugly. Jeers and shouted threats went up. Someone screamed, "hang him!" and others took up the call. Soon many in the crowd had joined the chant.

As T. J. and his procession passed a saloon the men suddenly surged forward and surrounded the killer's horse. Hands pulled at him trying to drag him from the saddle. T. J. wheeled the big buckskin around and heeled it into the men, driving them away from Amos Dutton.

Across the street Mary saw George Paxton's face turn grim. He quickly ducked into the Sheriff's office and emerged with a shotgun. Hurrying toward the enraged crowd he pointed the shotgun into the air and fired. The angry crowd immediately quieted and melted aside as he strode forward.

"You folks just settle down!" the sheriff shouted above the angry crowd. "Nobody's lynching nobody! I've got as much call to hate this man as anyone. He murdered my deputy. But he deserves a fair trial and I mean to see he gets it. Now stand aside!"

Mary drew a deep sigh of relief. It had been a tense moment. George had handled it well.

Pushing her way through the crowd she crossed the street and hurried to her husband as he was dismounting. He spotted her running toward him and opened his arms. She flung herself into his embrace. His strong arms wrapped around her so tightly she felt all but swallowed by his strength. Her grasping hands clutched at his neck, pulling his mouth to hers in a hungry kiss.

The bristle of his whiskered stubble ground into her chin but she paid it little mind. He was home.

"I'll take the prisoner off your hands," George said as T. J. and Mary finally broke the embrace. I expect you two have a lot to talk about."

"I expect," T. J. said, smiling at his friend. "I need you to sign this affidavit so I can collect the reward on Bob Dutton."

"Be glad to. Come on in the office and I'll take care of it then you can collect your money down at the bank."

"Where are the boys?" T. J. asked Mary.

"Probably wherever the Holly girls are. Do you need them?"

"Well, yeah. I need them to hitch up the wagon and pull it down to the store. There's something we need to pick up. Suppose you could have them do that while I drop by the bank?"

"Of course. I'll go find them."

"I'll be right along," he told her.

Mary found Tad and Lupe right where she expected she would, down by the creek with the Holly girls. She told them what T. J. had said and they left in a trot towards the livery. She visited with the girls for a few minutes then headed for the store. She couldn't imagine what it was T. J. needed to pick up.

She was almost to the store when she glanced down the street and saw T. J. walking toward her. She stopped to wait for him.

Suddenly a rifle shot rang out!

Her eyes flicked to the source of the sound at the end of the street, then back to her husband. T. J. arched high on his tiptoes. His shoulders drew back and the force of the bullet threw his chest forward. He staggered an awkward step, then sank slowly to his knees in the dusty street.

Mary saw all this even as a scream erupted from deep inside her being. Her feet carried her to him in a headlong run. He was lying on his face when she reached him. Somehow she managed to turn him over and cradle his head in her lap. She bent to press her face to his.

"Somebody get the Doctor!" a voice from somewhere shouted.

T. J.'s eyes fluttered open and found hers. Their gazes held each other for a long moment, their hearts in their eyes. Tears breached her eyelids and scorched hot trails down her cheeks. She could barely breathe.

"I love you," the words from his compressed lips were weak, barely above a whisper.

"I love you too," she choked out and pressed her lips to his.

"Anybody see who done this?" she heard the sheriff shout from somewhere nearby.

"Yeah," a voice from the crowd that had gathered shouted. "I was just coming into town and saw it. The shooter was a big fellow, looked more like a rancher than a back shooter. He lit out of town headed west with two more jaspers. He was riding the prettiest black stallion I ever laid eyes on."

"Get a posse together," the sheriff told someone. "We're going after them."

George knelt in the street beside T. J. "Don't worry, pard. We'll get them."

"Buck...Slade," T. J. whispered. "It was Buck Slade."

"That fellow you told me about from down in New Mexico?" George asked.

T. J. just gave a single nod of his head.

The Doctor arrived and knelt in the dirt. After a long moment's examination he raised his head slowly and looked at Mary. He sadly shook his head.

"George," T. J. said weakly. The sheriff knelt closer and bent an ear to hear the whispered words. "Watch after my family."

A shocked look swept across George Paxton's face. He flicked a look at Mary, then back at his friend. "You can count on it."

"P...pocket," T. J. barely managed from a failing voice.

The sheriff reached into T. J.'s shirt pocket and found a paper. He glanced at it briefly and handed it to Mary. With a puzzled look she read it. It was a receipt from the General Store for a stove, her stove, it was marked "Paid In Full."

A peaceful look crept slowly across T. J.'s face. He took a long shallow, shaky breath. Bloody froth bubbled on his lips. He gripped Mary's hand and squeezed it...and closed his eyes.

~THE END~

About the Author

Award-winning author, Dusty Rhodes was born in Eastern Oklahoma—formerly the notorious Indian Territory. Dusty grew up on stories of the old west. After retirement he began taking down those stories that had been gathering dust on the shelves of his mind and doing what he had dreamed of doing since childhood—writing historical westerns. His first book, Man Hunter, was named the best western e-book of 2002.